The Neoist Society

A subsidiary of the International Post-Dogmatist Group

Join us if you dare.

Neoist.org

Also by Cecil Touchon

Sell People Things They Don't Need
Is it Necessary to Say Something?
Happy Shopping
Important Documents of Post-Dogmatism
The Hidden Sphere of Artistic Concerns
Natural Born Fluxus
Fluxus Event Scores of Cecil Touchon
The Cut and Paste Poets – An Anthology of Collage Poetry

Additional Books from
Ontological Museum Publications

Massurrealism – Images, No Text - James Seefaher
A Room of Illusions - Alan King

Documents of Neoism:

The All New & Improved

Neoist Manifesto

(a trans-lingual edition)

With commentaries by Monty Cantsin and Karen Eliot

Edited by

Cecil Touchon

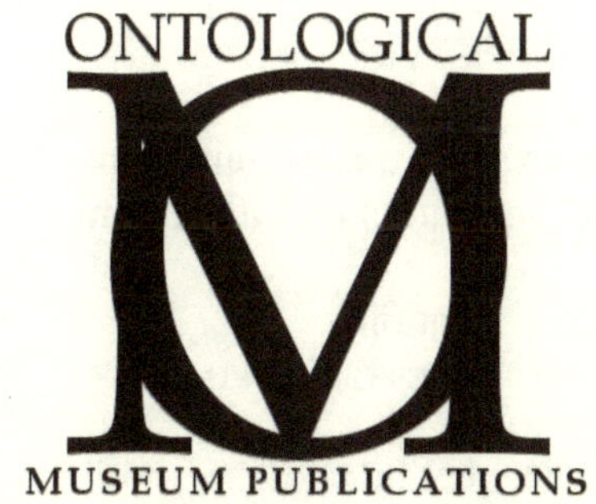

Ontological Museum Publications
Ontologicalmuseum.org

Cover Image: Fusion Series #2318 © 2007 by Cecil Touchon
Cover Design: © 2008 by Cecil Touchon

The illustrations in this book are all images of collages on paper by Cecil Touchon and are a part of his Fusion Series that he has been working on since 1983. See Touchon's website at touchon.com

ISBN: 978-0-615-25881-2
First Paperback Edition

Ontological Museum Publications
For contact information visit us online at:
Ontologicalmuseum.org

Table of Contents

Acknowledgements

The Neoist Society would like to thank the staff at Ontological Museum Publications who believed in this project from its inception. We would also like to thank our brothers-in-arms: the International Post Dogmatist Group for their continued support and encouragement.

What Neoism is and How You can be a Part of It

Neoism is an artistic rather than scientific approach to life. It is an open approach not dependant on provability to anyone other than yourself.

First of all, Neoism is based on laws of formation and dissolution, of mass influences, and environmental limitations. Neoists find new ways of communication. The important thing is that Neoism has decided to make life fun and we take our fun seriously.

Second, Neoism tends to destroy rigorous, precise, and tested rules, every Neoists is free to follow his own impulses. In this he will show his genius or lack thereof.

Third, one type of Neoism will be found suitable in one situation and completely useless in another. To undertake an active Neoist operation, it is not necessary to make a scientific, sociological and psychological analysis first. Proper training is not necessary for those who want to use Neoist research to full effectiveness.

Finally, one last trait reveals the artistic character of Neoism: it does not depend on external controls or criteria, it is not concerned with standards of success and failure, it remains undefined in its goals. A Neoist is prompted by a certain internal impulse to experimentation and a desire to ponder.

The Individual and the Masses

Neoism will address itself at one and the same time to the individual and the masses. It cannot separate the two elements. For Neoism to address itself to the individual, in his isolation, apart from the crowd, is very possible. The individual, as an isolated unit, is of great interest to the Neoist Society. To win people over one by one is a typical Neoist Society strategy. Neoism begins where simple dialogue begins.

A Neoism that functioned only where individuals are gathered together would be incomplete and insufficient. Neoism reaches individuals yet it also aims at a crowd, but only as a body understood to be composed of individuals. When addressing the crowd, the Neoist thinks of it on whole as if a single individual for, in fact, all of humanity together is nothing more than many individual expressions of but a single being dreaming of itself as many.

The individual is considered in terms of what unique characteristics he has, such as his motivations, his feelings, or his myths. The individual is never considered as part of a mass of many different people because in that way his psychic defenses are stronger, his reactions are faster and more provocative, and he is less prone to identify a message as being directed exactly at him. But the individual must never be considered as being alone; the listener to a pirate radio broadcast, though actually alone, is nevertheless part of a large group, and he is aware of it.

Pirate radio listeners have been found to exhibit a kind of terrorist mentality. All are tied together and constitute a sort of underground society in which all individuals are accomplices though they may never meet any other members of the group that they believe themselves to be a part of.

When Neoism is addressed to a crowd, it must touch each individual in that crowd. To be effective, it must give the impression of being personal, for we must never forget that the masses are composed of individuals, and is in fact nothing but assembled individuals.

When individuals are in a group, their individuality is weakened, they enter a state of receptivity, and are in a state of psychological regression yet they pretend all the more to be strong individuals. The crowd as an organism is clearly subhuman but pretends to give superhuman qualities to its members.

Thus Neoism profits from the structure of the mass, but exploits the individual's need for self-affirmation. Neoism has precisely this remarkable effect of reaching the whole crowd all at once, and yet reaching each individual in that crowd.

The movie spectator, though elbow to elbow with his neighbors, is always alone, separated by the darkness and the hypnotic attraction of the screen. This is the situation of the "lonely crowd", or of isolation in the mass, which is a natural product of present-day hi-tech society and which is both used and deepened by Neoism.

The most favorable moment to seize the attention and influence a potential participant is when he is alone in the crowd: it is at this point that Neoism can be most effective.

Total Neoism and Neoist Propaganda Methods

Neoism must be total. Neoists may utilize all of the technical means at their disposal - graffiti, stickers, mail-art, networking, music, Internet, video, DVD, computers, telephones, texting devices, painting, sculpture, poetry, novels, smoke signals, exhibitions, collage, montage, etc. There is no Neoism as long as one makes use, in sporadic fashion and at random, of a manifesto here, a poster or a radio program there, organizes a few apartment festivals and network meetings, writes a few slogans on the walls; that is not enough. Each usable medium has its own particular way of limited penetration. A video does not play on the same motives, does not produce the same feelings, and does not provoke the same reactions as a poster. The very fact that the effectiveness of each medium is limited to one particular area clearly shows the necessity of complementing it with other media available. A word spoken on the radio is not the same, does not produce the same effect, and does not have the same impact as the identical word spoken in private conversation at an apartment festival or in a public speech before a large crowd at a stadium. To draw the individual into net of Neoism, each technique must be utilized in its own specific way, directed toward producing the effect it can best produce, and fuse with all the other media, each of them reaching the individual in a specific fashion and making him react anew to the same theme - in the same direction, but differently.

Human contact is the best medium for the spreading of the Neoist agenda in terms of social climate, fast infiltration, progressive inroads, and over-all integration. Public meetings and posters are more suitable tools for providing shock effect, intense but temporary, leading to immediate action. The press tends more to shape general views; radio and TV are likely to be instruments of international action and impregnation of the psycho-mental sphere known as the Massurreality, whereas the press is used locally and domestically. In any case, it is understood that because of this specialization not one of these instruments may be left out: they must all be used in combination.

We are here in this world in the presence of a self organizing reality that already controls the formation of the entire universe. We merely are creating a mythic version of it to facilitate our ability to communicate to each other about it and help to shape our expression of it. Through the myth it creates, Neoism imposes a complete range of intuitive knowledge. Intuitive knowledge - being ambiguous – is susceptible to multi-sided interpretation.

This myth – due to the primal nature to which it refers - becomes so powerful that it invades every area of communication, leaving no faculty or motivation unaffected. It stimulates in the individual a feeling of all inclusiveness. Neoism has such motivational force that it engages the whole of the individual.

This explains the totalitarian attitude that the Neoist adopts where ever Neoism has successfully been inculcated.

Everything can serve as a means of Neoist propaganda and everything must be utilized.

Continuity and Duration of Neoism

Neoism is continuous and everlasting - continuous in that it leaves no gaps, but fills the Neoist´s whole day and all his days; everlasting in that it functions into the incalculable future.

Neoism occupies every moment of the Neoist's life, at home, in the street, at the dentist, in a bar or in bed. Its base is a constant impregnation of the impulses of the Now into the mind of the Neoist. It creates convictions and compliance through imperceptible influences.

Neoism is a complete environment for the Neoist master from which he never escapes.

Neoism is not a stimulus that disappears quickly; it consists of successive impulses and shocks aimed at various feelings or thoughts. As soon as one effect wears off, it is followed by a new shock.

The Now is always surprising. Thus the content of Neoism can seem so inconsistent that it can approve today what it condemned yesterday. Monty Cantsin considers this changeability of Neoism an indication of its confusing nature. Actually it is only an indication of the grip it exerts, of the reality of its effects.

Neoism continues its assault without an instant's respite. The Now is forever just now happening and the Neoists are there to participate in it.

Organization of Neoism

Neoism is self arising, self organizing and self correcting thus it must not be organized along any particular rule. Though Neoism negates the need of a centralized administrative organization, each practitioner of Neoism is the administrator of his own activities. The practice of Neoism is tied to the realities of the everyday life of each practitioner which spawn the specific rules of construction of all individual Neoist actions and activities.

Neoism cannot operate from inside of a vacuum cleaner (at least not while it is running). This is a principal conviction of Monty Cantsin.

Neoism operates through the dismissal of the past and the promise of a future - an effective way of counter-propaganda. Thus the apparatus of Neoism removes the people from a reliance on past traditions that lose weight on the treadmill of argument.

Neoism then, is practice. Practice furnishes the Neoist with vital reasons, juicy justifications, and rejuvenating motivations for continuing his daily neoist activities and refining his wakefulness.

Each must act with sincerity as if they believe in what they are doing. This is the only way to find complete satisfaction in Neoism

Each Neoist is a representative of the holographic organization that is the Neoist Society: each is a complete Neoist Society in himself; a self-sufficient shard of the greater body of the Neoist Society. Monty Cantsin is the greater body of which each Neoist is a part, his personage casting the long shadow of Neoism. Each has an inner knowing that lets him know why he speaks certain words and what effect they should have. His words are no longer human words but hyper-words of entirely spontaneous ideas to reflect the structure of the Neoist Society. When necessary he can turn in the opposite direction and act with similar conviction should the New require him to move thusly. He must believe only in the arising Newness and not be bogged down by the past – even if it were just a moment ago - in order to remain fluid.

No, Monty Cantsin will never become the prisoner of his own formulas. What protects him is his exact and precise adherence to the principles of the New and the Neoist Society to which he belongs. The Neoist Society never promotes rigidity and we are very firm about that.

The Orthopraxic Cure

Neoism is very frequently described as a conspiracy of the New for the purpose of replacing old ideas or opinions, with new and better ideas and opinions. Neoism is based on an intuitive response to the ever arising New rather than a reasoned building up of traditional beliefs into an edifice of logical stupidity.

Once awakened, the Neoist's first response to this misshapened body of incongruities is to make fun of it, through parody and mocking: to then abandon its false order and raise up nonsense in its place but this is only to add braces and prosthetic devices to a disfigured tragedy that is the result of accidental conditions.

This is much of what we have seen in Neoism till now. This line of reasoning is completely wrong: To view Neoism as still being what it was in 1960 is to cling to an obsolete concept; it is to condemn oneself to understand nothing about Neoism.

To cleave to the ever arising New is to create a firm adherence to truth and to negate everything else. If one's sincerity is sufficiently strong; one's intuitions sufficiently clear then, after some soul searching, the individual is ready for the destruction of the edifice of belief he has falsely groomed as his self, leading to the possibility of being an awakened Neoist - the most dangerous creature alive.

The aim of Neoism is to open the door, leave the cage and learn to fly.

Neoism aims solely at the artful participation of the free and awakened Neoist in the everyday life all around him sometimes passively sometimes through action.

To be effective, Neoism must constantly short circuit all artificial thought and mechanical decision making processes. Neoism has meaning only when it obtains the convergence of the ever arising internal impulses, with the artful expression of the Neoist. Neoism must at once operate on the individual at the superficial level of the ultraconscious in concert with the profoundly internal intuitive knowing.

The individual knows that he is being shaped by the internal forces of Now while bringing refinements to that shaping with his growing knowledge of Neoism without care about the release of that knowledge that will provide the appropriate action at the appropriate moment.

Through telepathic transmission emitted by the Masters of the Neoist Society through the infinitely arising Present, the proselyte receives an overwhelming impulse that makes him awaken the whole of his being to the New and to the Now. He is transformed into a lion in a psycho-sociological sense.

Action by an awakened Neoist makes Neoism's effect irresistible. The awakened Neoist can never return to that life that went before when he lived in a random poorly constructed dream of someone else's making. He is now obliged for his own good through his Neoist wakefulness to uphold Neoist practice. He is obliged to continue to advance in the direction indicated by the Neoist impulses arising within him. Starting demands continuing. The individual who has acted in accordance with Neoism has taken up his place in the Neoist Society. From then on, old farts hanging onto the past make themselves his enemies. Often the power of his connection to newness causes an estrangement with what had been previously established. He starts to recognize new friends that the Neoist Society has made for him. He is caught up in a movement that totally occupies his consciousness. Neoism and the Now occupies him completely and we must bear in mind that if Neoism leads to this kind of participation it is child's play – the very best kind of play.

In order for a Neoist to become a master a certain amount of time must elapse, a period of training and conditioning. One cannot hope to obtain subtle reactions to the ever arising impulses of the Now after only a few weeks' practice. A real psychic reformation of priorities must be undertaken, so that after months of patient work a Neoist will react automatically in the hoped-for direction to his inner impulses. What is visible in Neoism, what is spectacular and seems to us often incomprehensible or unbelievable, is possible only because of such slow preparation; without it nothing would be possible. Be patient and persistent.

The aspiring Neoist creates myths by which, he at first and later many people, will live by. By myth we mean a cult-activating total image: a sort of vision of primal ambiguous objectives, practical in character that have over-whelming, all-encompassing influences on the surrounding community. Such an image inspires the Neoist to action precisely because it includes all that he feels is direct, compelling and incomprehensible in its spreading power. Eventually the myth takes possession of the Neoist's mind so completely that his life is consecrated to it. Neoists create and live in a collective milieu of myth.

Join us if you dare.

The Neoist Society
Neoist.org

The All New & Improved
Neoist Manifesto

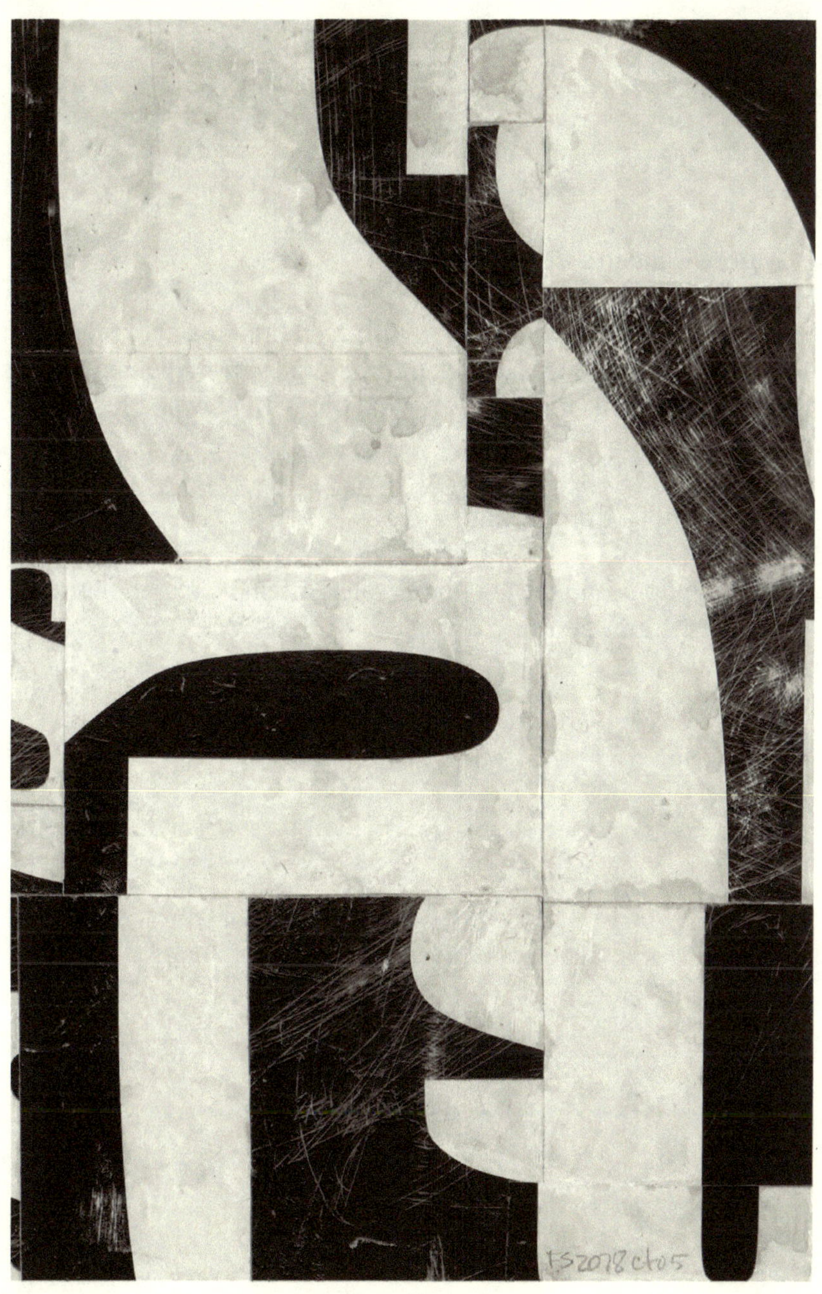

Plate 1

1

Monty Cantsin's Commentary:

The Neoist draws in the Now with each breath and expresses the New with each impulse. His intuition rises from the heart of his being, enters his mind and fills his life with new and renewing energy.

Karen Eliot's Commentary

Barking dogs and the sound of water: attempts to geometricise post-structural desire.

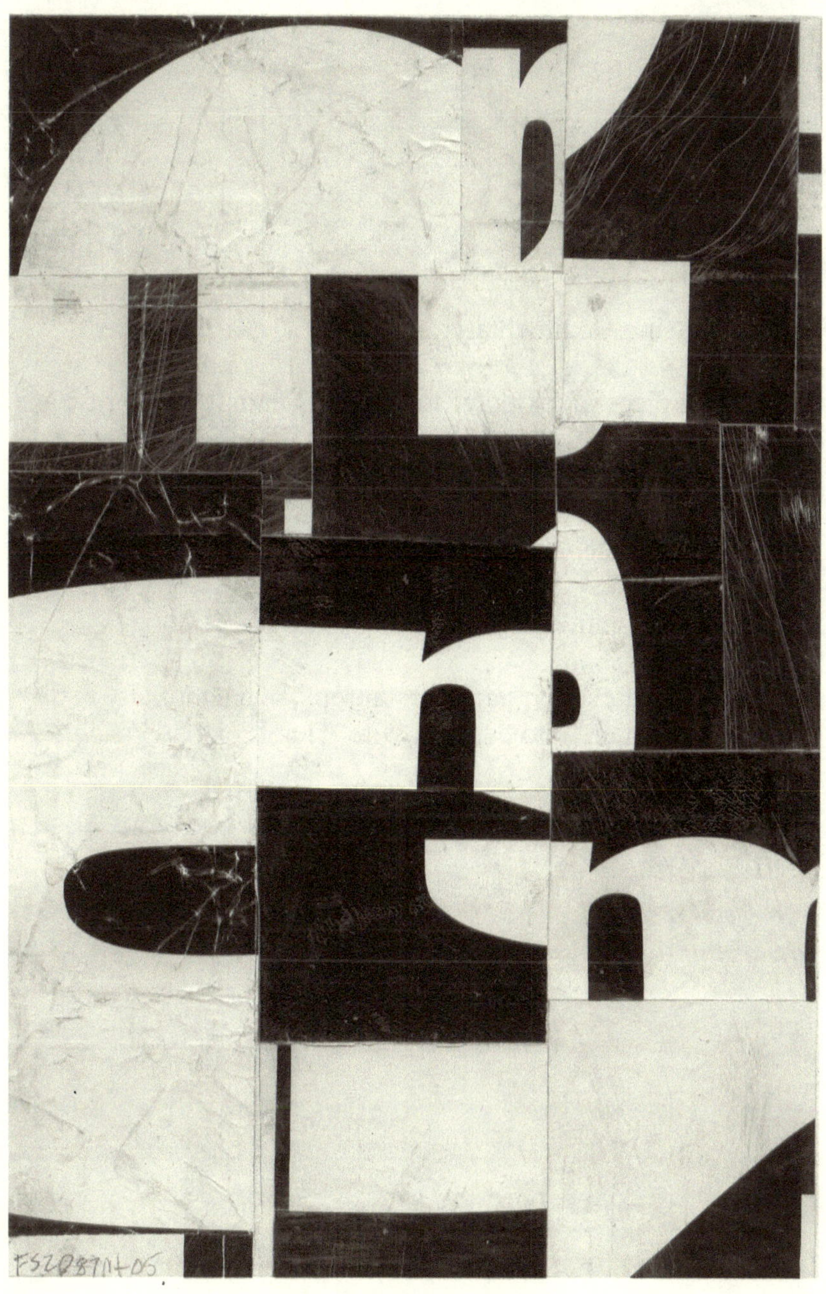

Plate 2

Monty Cantsin's Commentary:

Why does a piece of text have to have sequentially, linearity, and originality to be considered "meaningful?" The hostile reaction of the critic seems to indicate that these are far from dead issues, he struggles so valiantly to extract "meaning" out of a text that had been deliberately rendered "meaningless."

Karen Eliot's Commentary

The concerns of energy, particles, entropy, and continuity to the rendering of culture into everyday life. That is one approach.

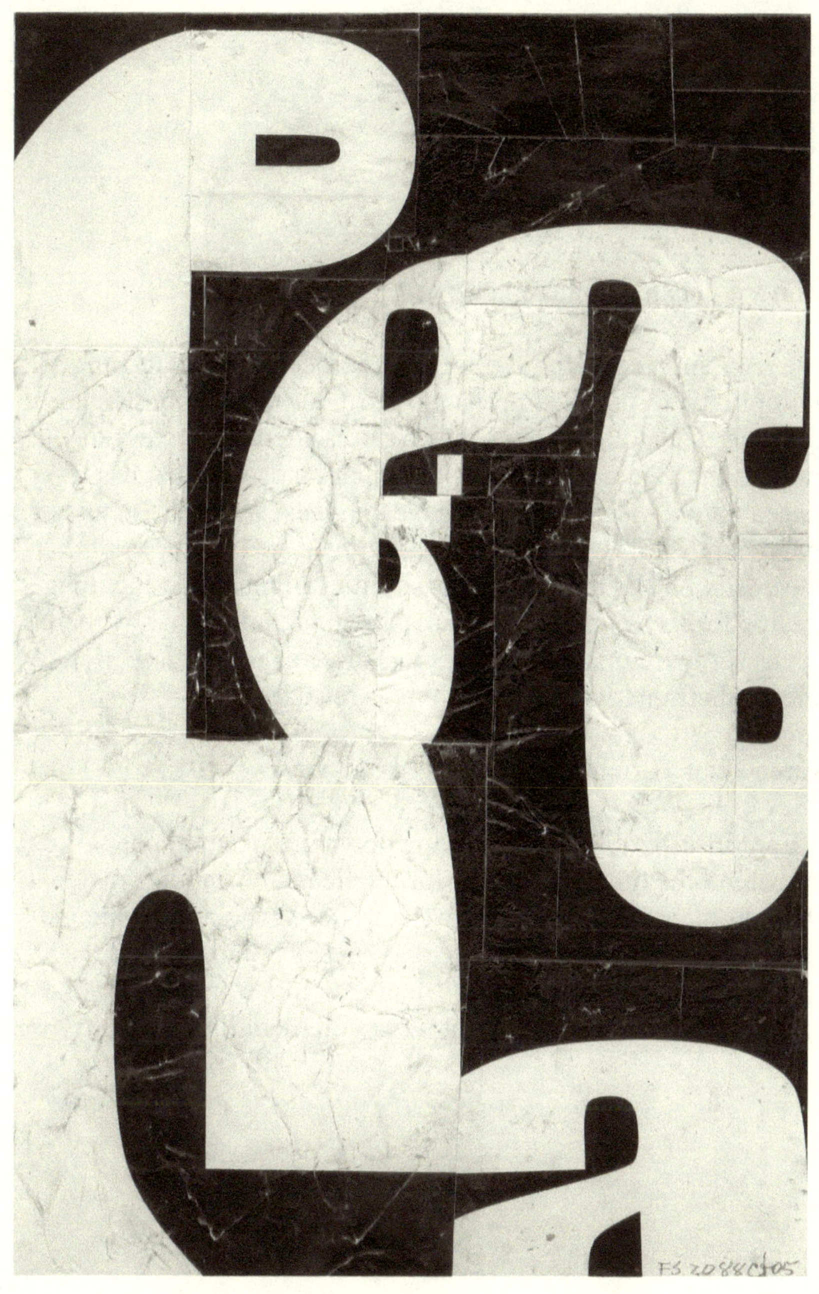

Plate 3

3

Monty Cantsin's Commentary:

The recycling, editing, rearranging, reprocessing and reusing of multiplicity, of political propaganda, of corporate commercial messages and cultural signs that are presented to us every day through the media - the new spectacular landscape that has replaced nature - is an art form that can release intuitive impulses that reconnect us with our primal origins.
We open ourselves up to the possibilities of manipulating images created for us by capital rather than being manipulated by them. Let us set these images and messages free as we are free. Let us release their internal power as ours is released.

Karen Eliot's Commentary

We are insufferably elitist looking down our noses at people so far behind the times as to look for intellectual meanings in a text. Our commentaries are for the weak minded who need someone to hold their hand. Whatever we say means nothing. Read the All New and Improved Neoist Manifesto like a painting or like music! That is the manifesto, not our commentary!

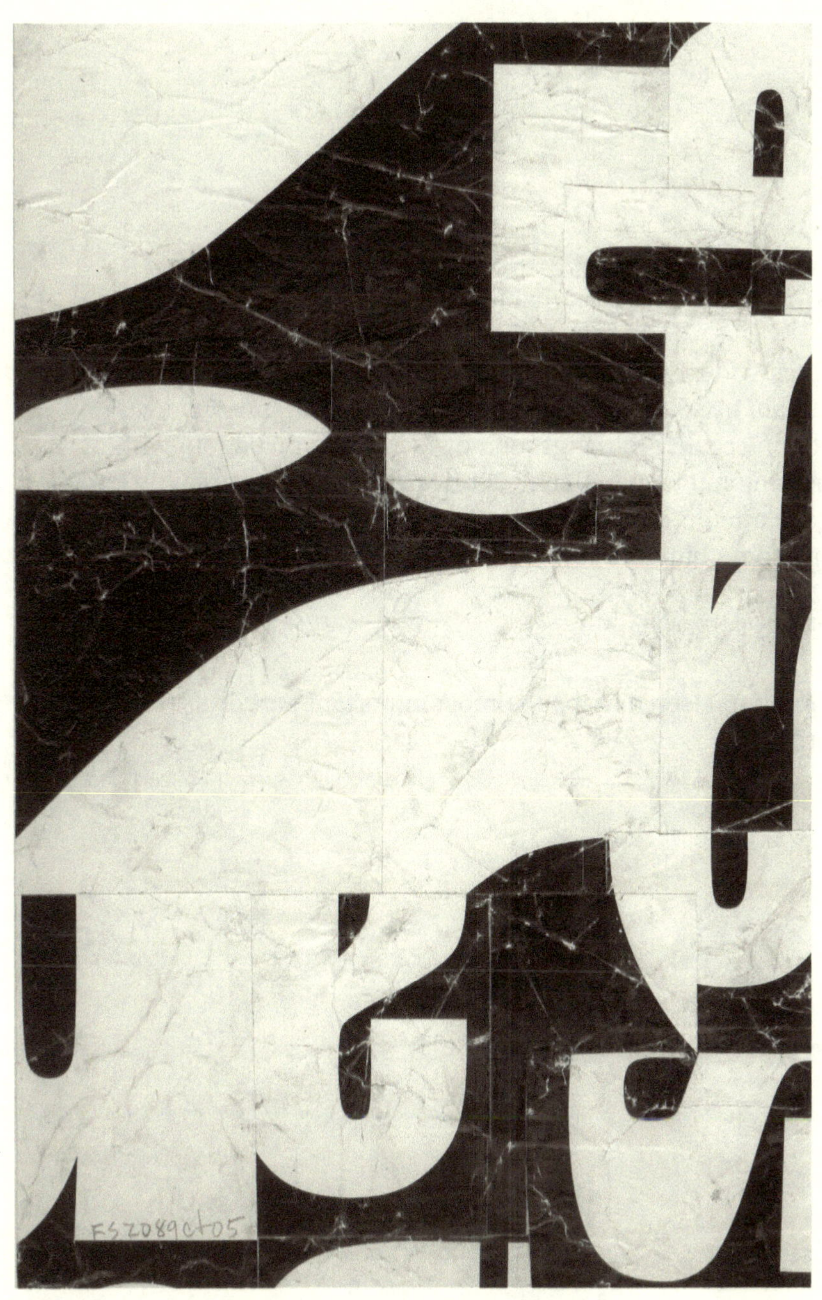

Plate 4

4

Monty Cantsin's Commentary:

Even wide awake with an obsessive attention to detail, even a certain urgency, try to pin down the ever arising and ever dissolving reality to the ground of facts and you end up with nothing but unexplainable stories and incomprehensible knowledge attempting to be semi profound. So is it really necessary to say something? If not, remain silent.

Karen Eliot's Commentary

Going to sleep may be the most important part of the creative process.

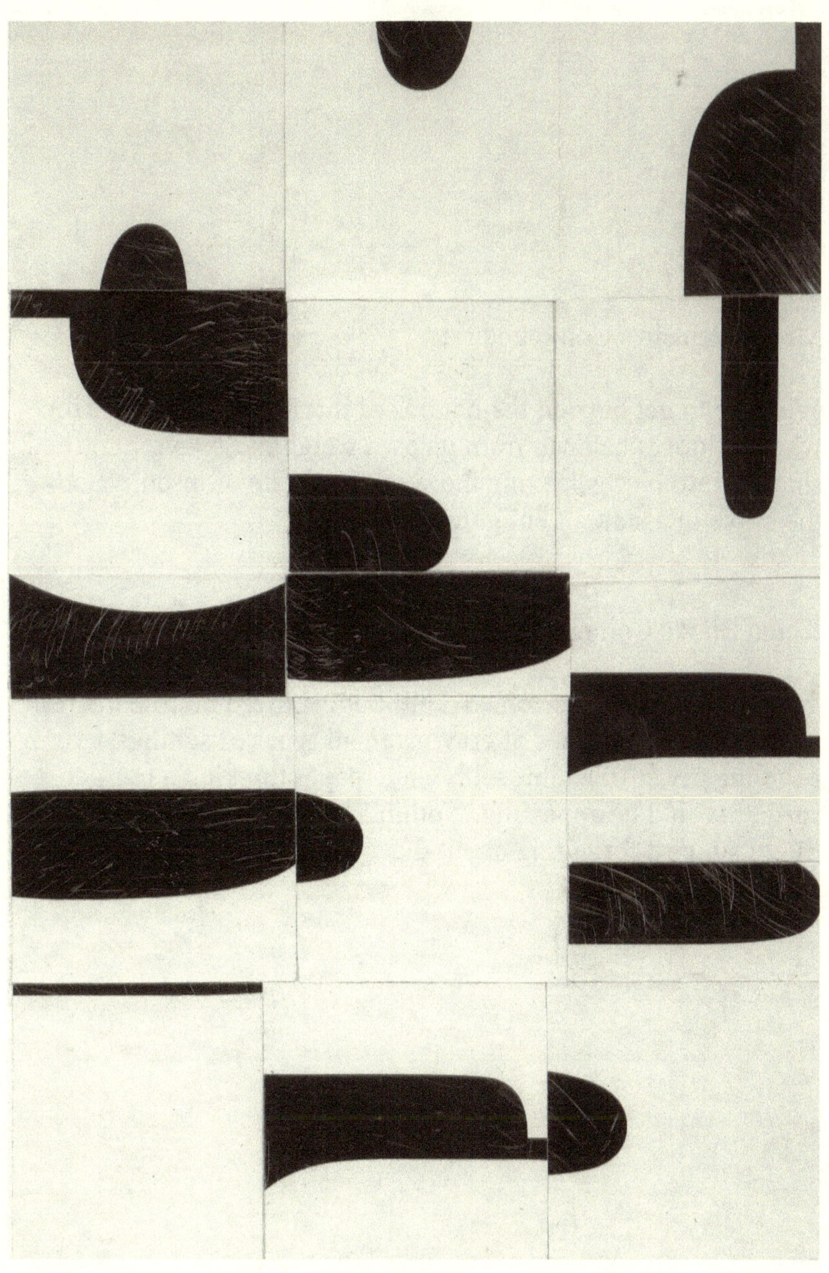

Plate 5

Monty Cantsin's Commentary:

We have to get beyond the bounds of information, into a realm where it looses balance from its own weightiness, overturns and shatters into pieces leaving the weak in a state of insanity and the brave in a state of enlightenment.

Karen Eliot's Commentary

When I was three I scribbled a bit, but I showed no true interest in it. I've tried all types of crayons in all types of settings, even covering my coffee table with white paper thinking a big flat surface would be appealing. Nothing.
May I suggest forgetting about the crayons.

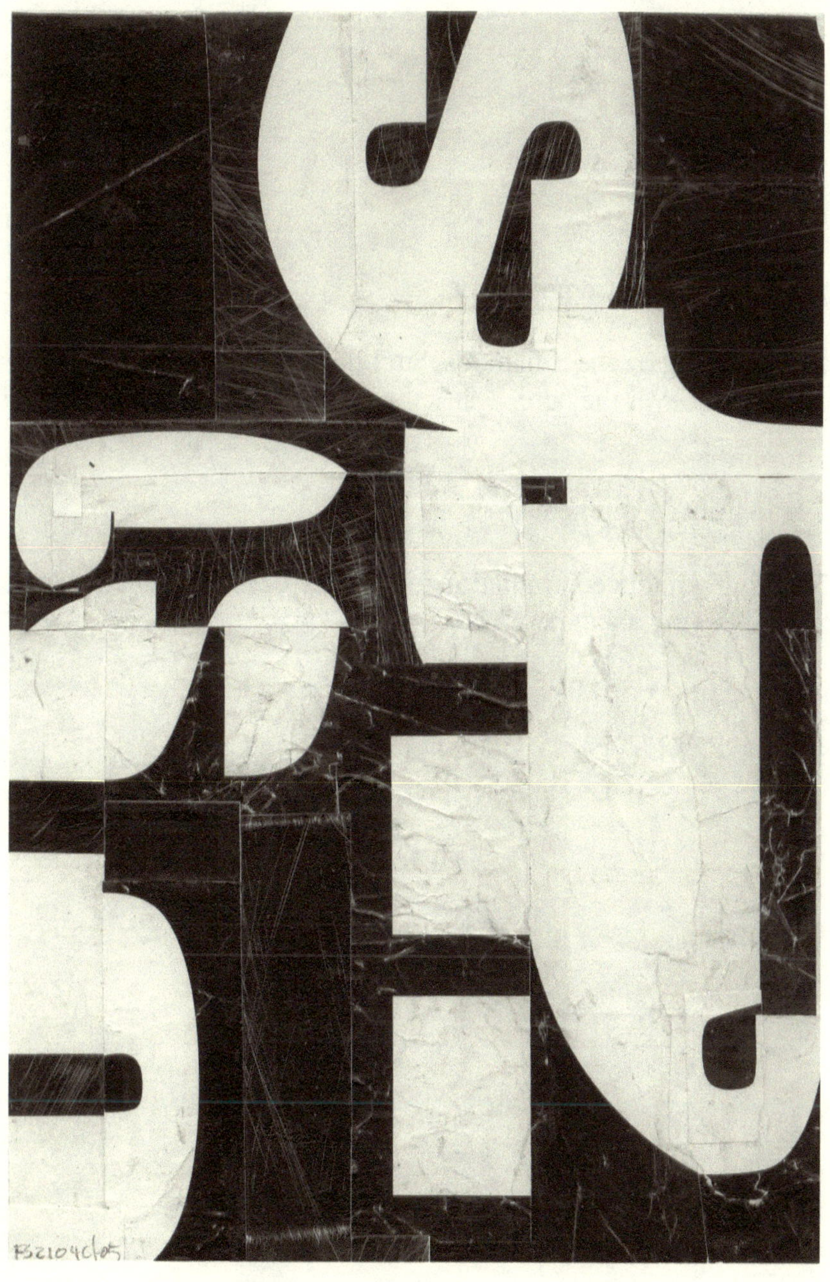

Plate 6

6

Monty Cantsin's Commentary:

It's bordering on the ridiculous, but I don't mind them using my name - whoever they are. That's the nature of this game.

Karen Eliot's Commentary

Meaning without contradiction to the state of the Present is what we are talking about here.

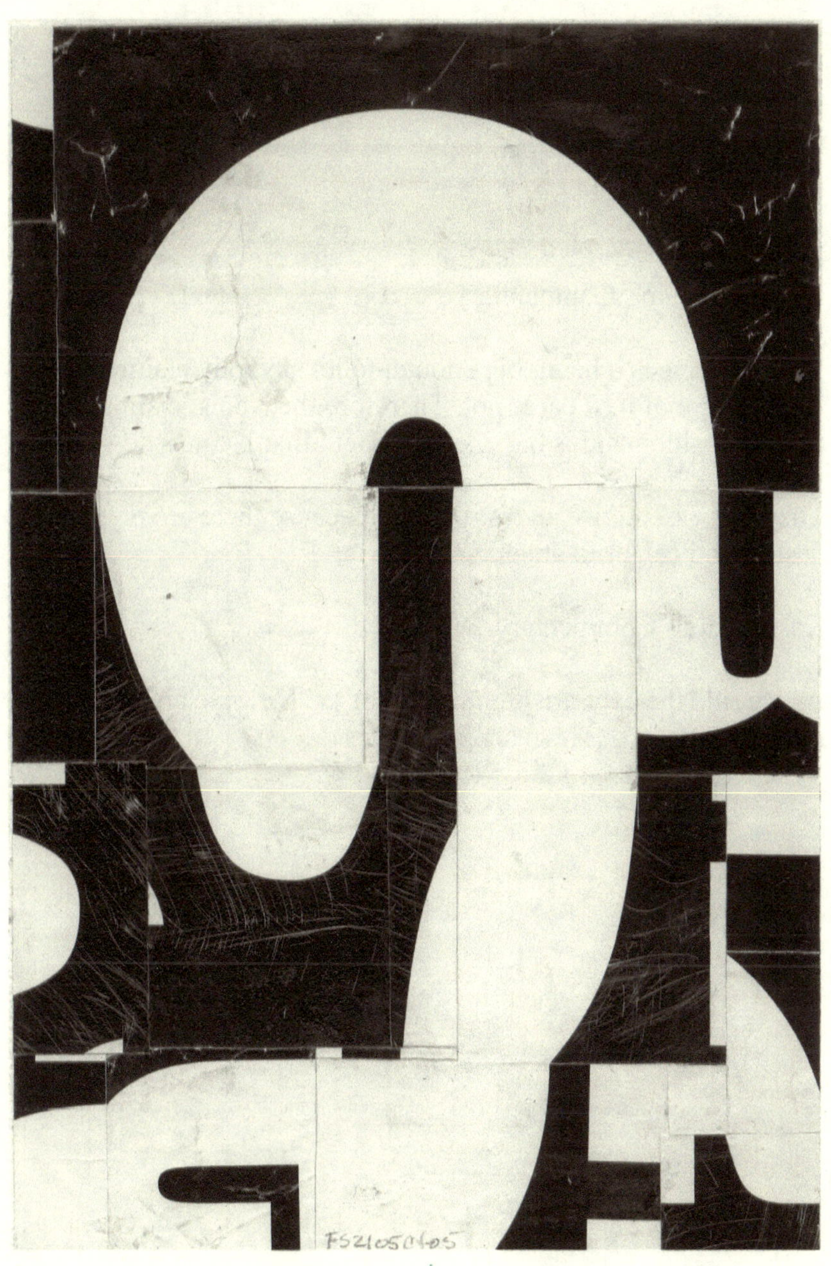

Plate 7

7

Monty Cantsin's Commentary:

The Universe is a being big enough to let anybody claim that he is the centre of it. It cares not. Therefore the Neoist claims this central position and is big enough to let other Neoists do so as well.
They are, essentially, indestructible, because there are no parts to destroy, no center to attack.

Karen Eliot's Commentary

As we ride the ever arising impulse of the New we are the ghosts that haunt us in our own artificial lives.

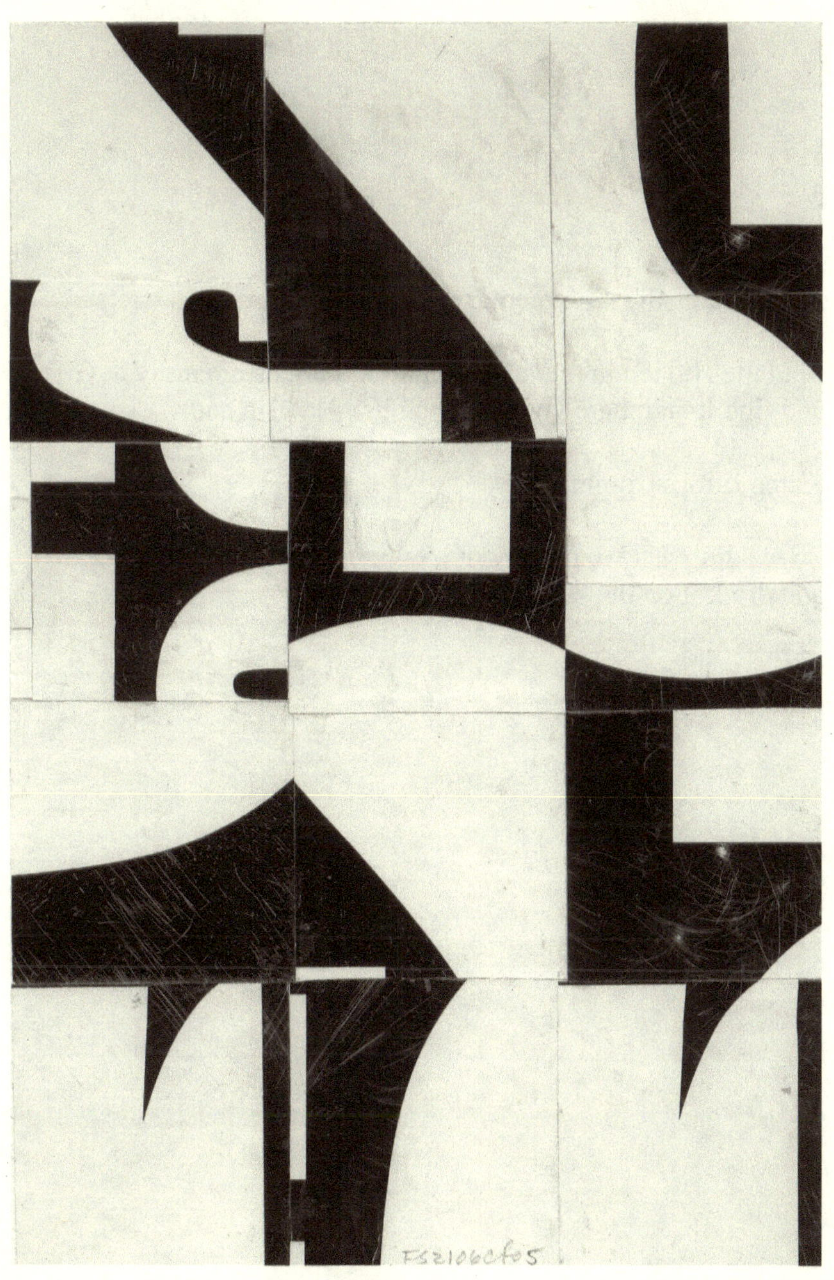

Plate 8

8

Monty Cantsin's Commentary:

Find the Hidden in the failing light of a circus or carnival. Go and find it and there you will establish Neoism anew.

Karen Eliot's Commentary

So we did what we usually did, purchased a bottle of Tequila and drink it on the back terrace.

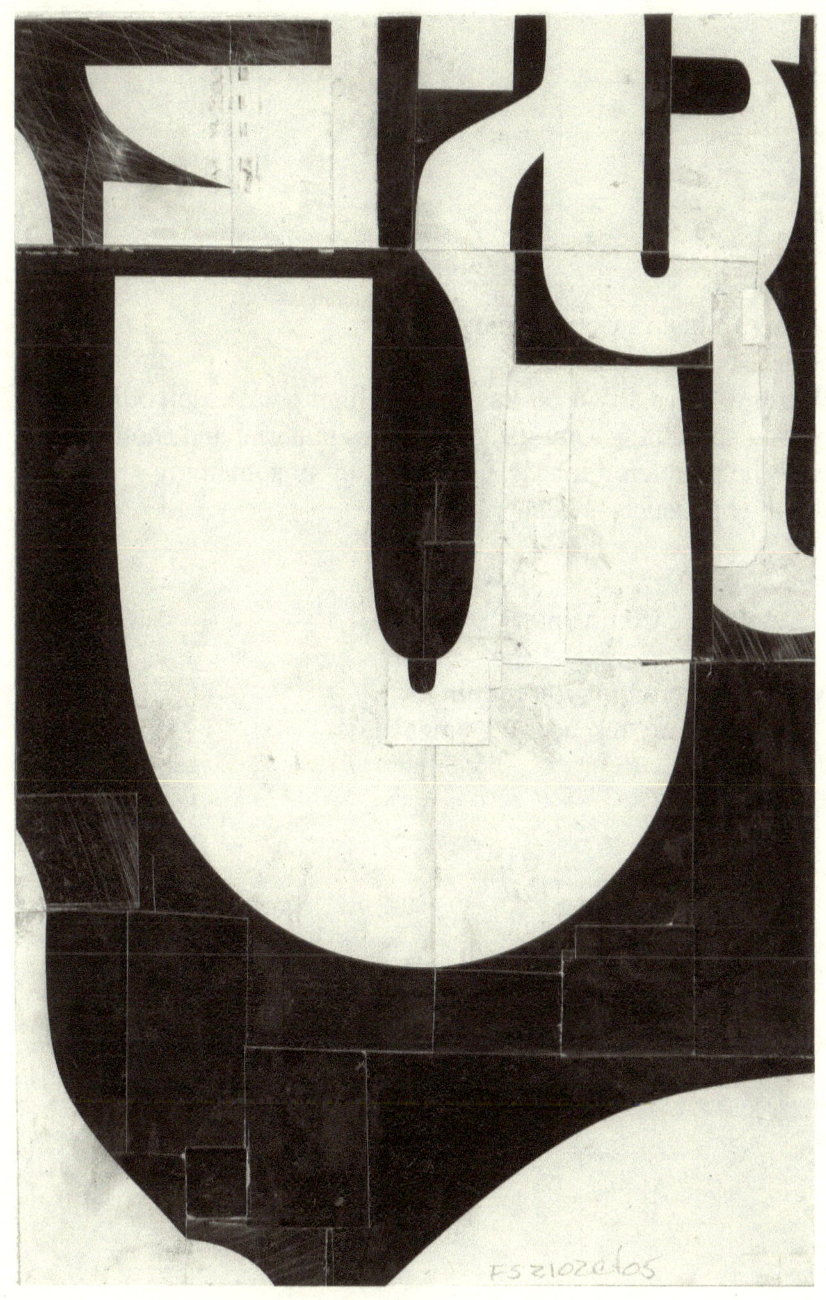

Plate 9

9

Monty Cantsin's Commentary:

Words as normally used - as ways to manipulate each other into buying something - are insignificant as material and should always be plundered for their parts in hunt of something worthwhile, such as beauty.

Karen Eliot's Commentary

My scream brought you running.
I called you my rescuer. We laughed.

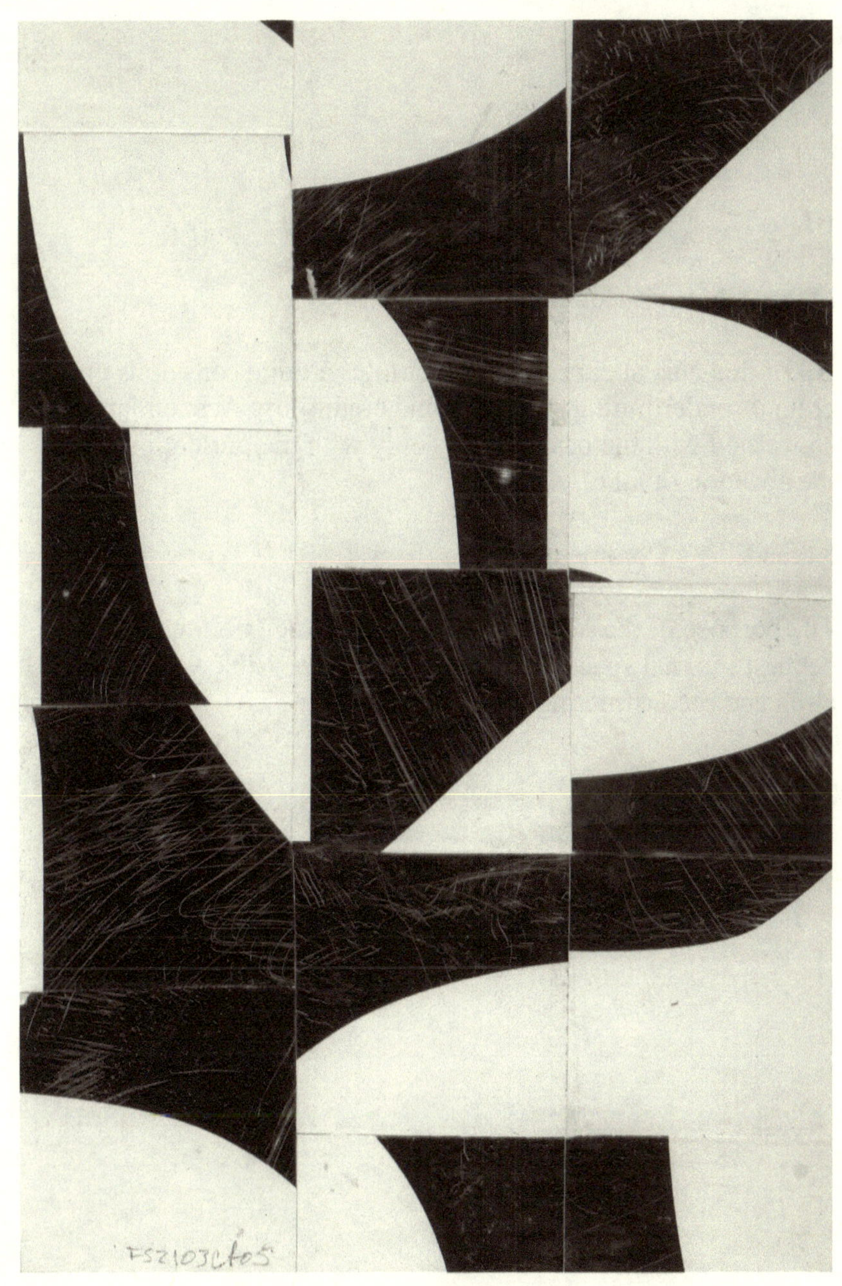

Plate 10

Monty Cantsin's Commentary:

All of this Neoist expression constitutes a quite conscious program of undermining any academic credibility. Academians are concerned with the past, Neoists only with the present intent to the abandon of all else.

Karen Eliot's Commentary

The purpose of the poet is exposing just exactly Now from the deepest internal spaces in the newest way possible while recycling and reconstructing the past.

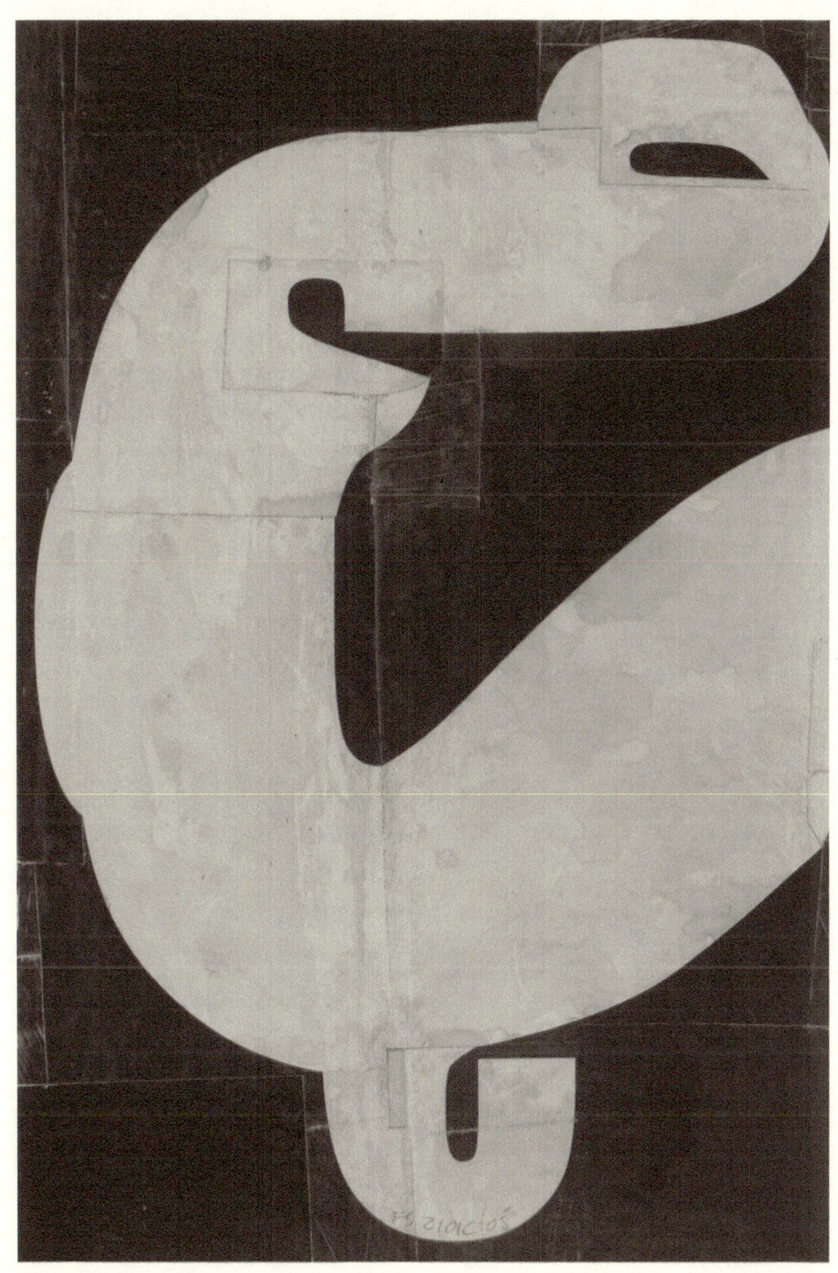

Plate 11

11

Monty Cantsin's Commentary:

You can cover you head or blow it out your ass but Neoism arrived before everything else and shall remain after all else is gone.

Karen Eliot's Commentary

All in spotless petticoats ruffling, remnants of lives lived to the limit and then cast aside with nonchalance and abandon.

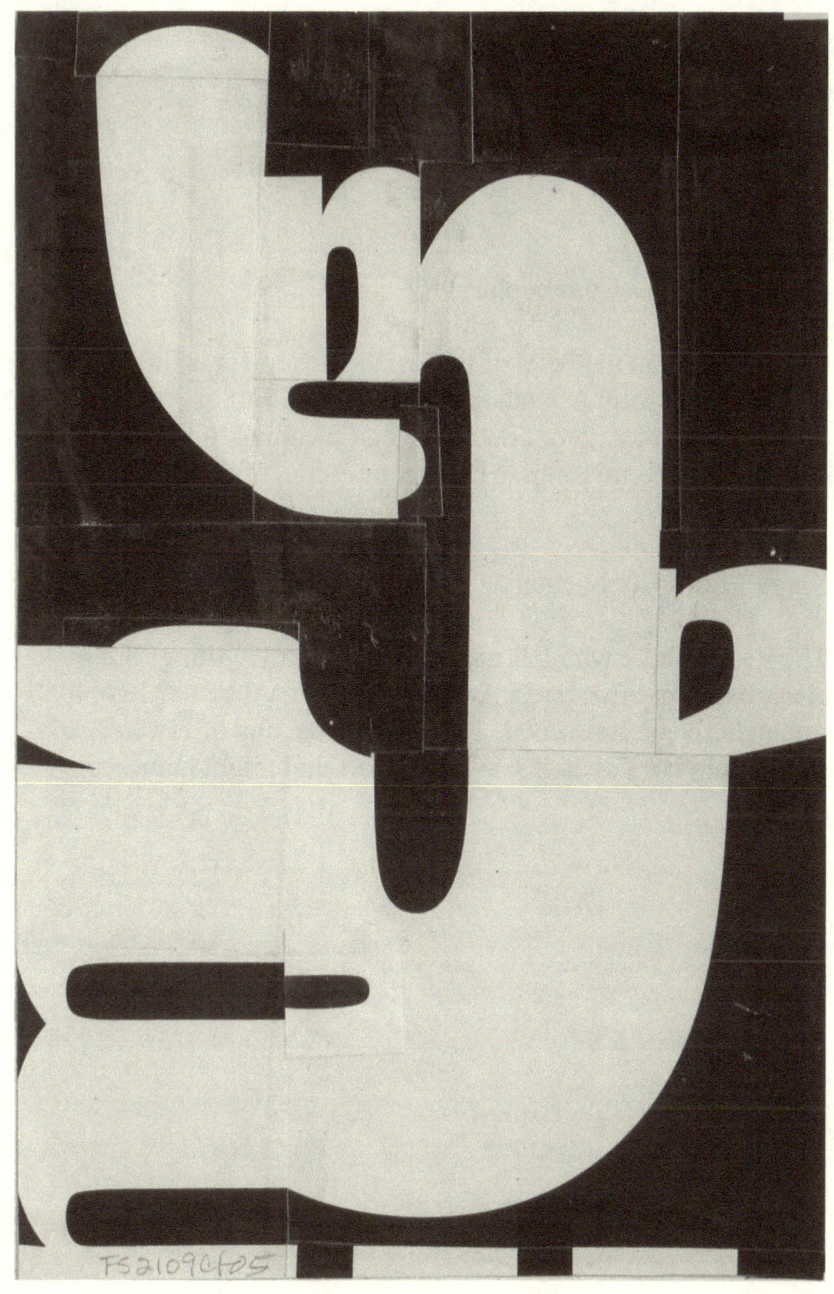

Plate 12

Monty Cantsin's Commentary:

One of the main methods of the artists of Neoism is the idea that anyone could form a band or make a work of art or write a poem or, for that matter, give new shape and meaning to Neoism without anyone's permission. Whose permission, after all, would one seek?

Karen Eliot's Commentary

There are people who tell me that some of my writings are plagiarisms of my own texts. And why wouldn't they be? I got it all somewhere else anyway. If I actually wrote any of my work myself I could not now tell you which part that might have been.

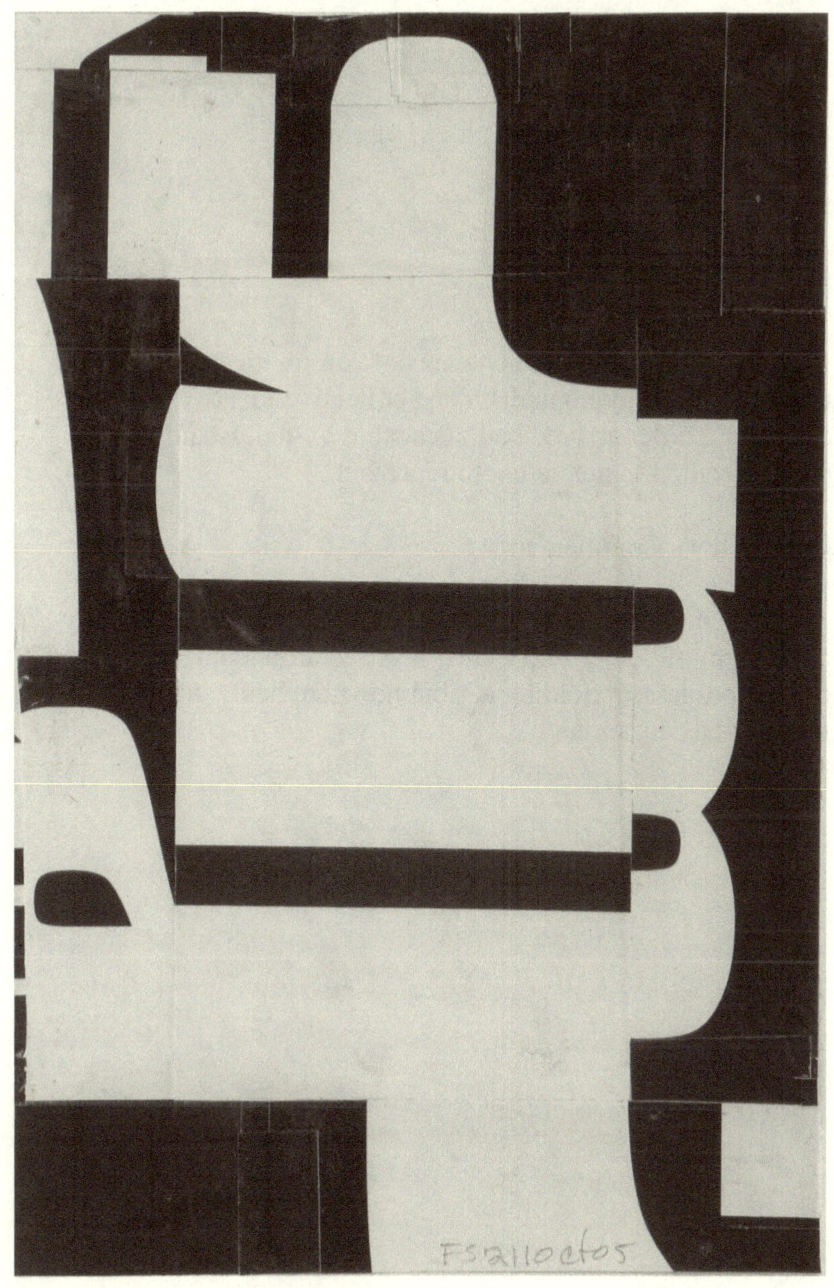

Plate 13

13

Monty Cantsin's Commentary:

Identity and fixity are the enemies of communication and have to be combated by nomadism and collective identity. The forces of law and order arrived and, incapable of understanding the event, decided immediately to repress it.

Karen Eliot's Commentary

The Neoist having no prior cause, cannot be contained by any other form of being. The Neoist is orbed around all; possessing, but not possessed, holding all, but nowhere held: all that is unfailing finds duration.

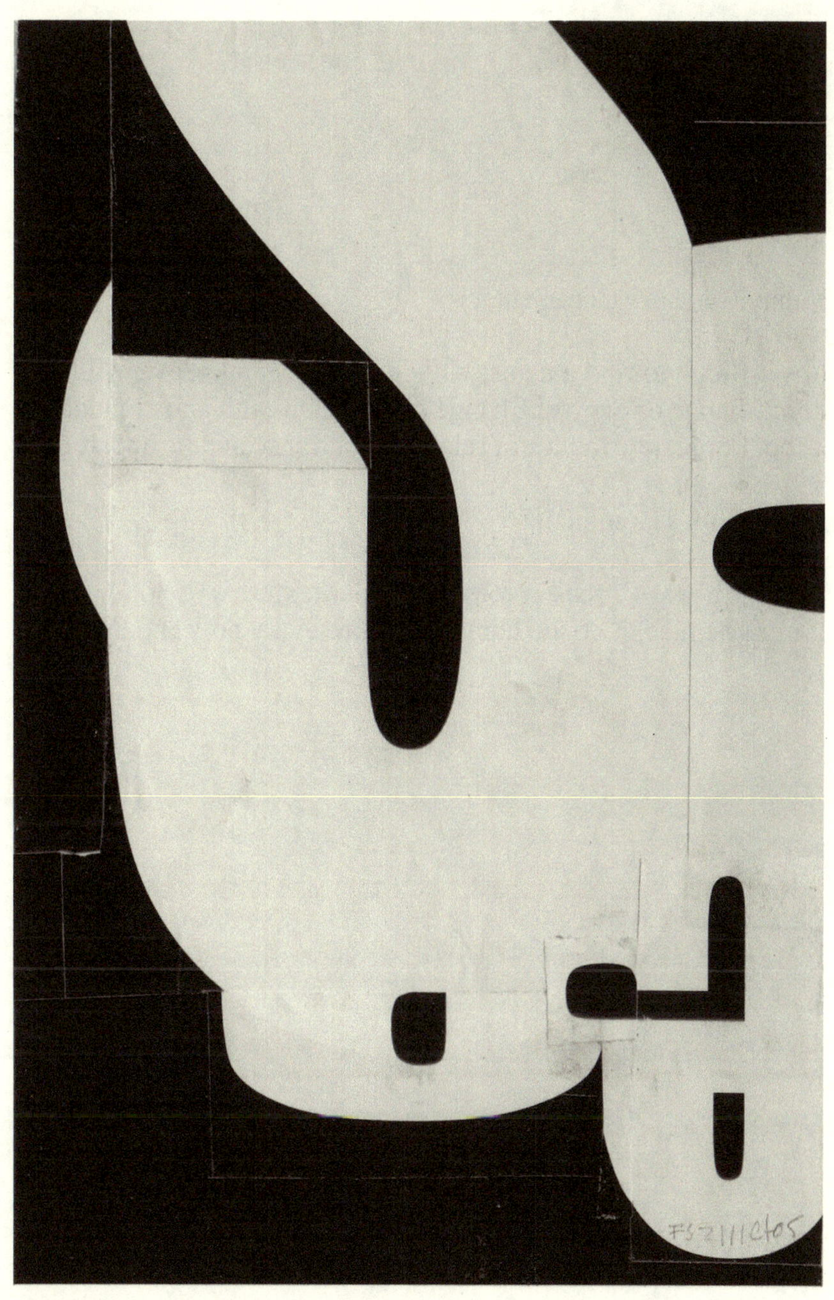

Plate 14

Monty Cantsin's Commentary:

It is difficult to find a neoist who is equally good at every function. Change or evolve. Change generates wealth and circulates it too. Forge new modes of relating that transcend the apparent.

Karen Eliot's Commentary

There is always a reason for a particular texture or color.
It must be nice to be the hometown hero every now and then.

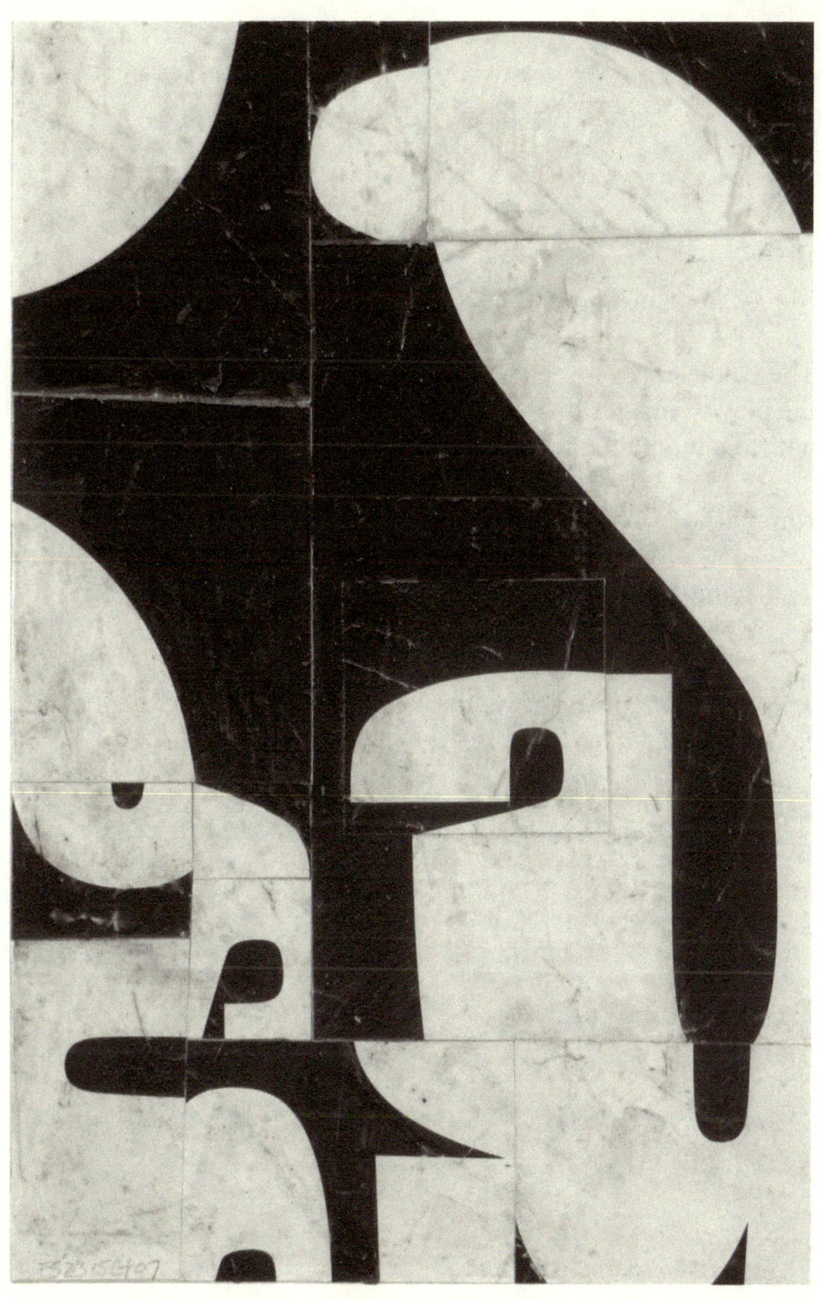

Plate 15

15

Monty Cantsin's Commentary:

The whole core of the conundrum, the enigma, the subtlety and the play of images that intersected his elaborate collages have, not for a moment, dreamt of hiding.

Karen Eliot's Commentary

To begin with, I love the effect of light and magnificent, awe-inspiring peace.

The Neoists know what we think and feel, what we experience. So do we all.

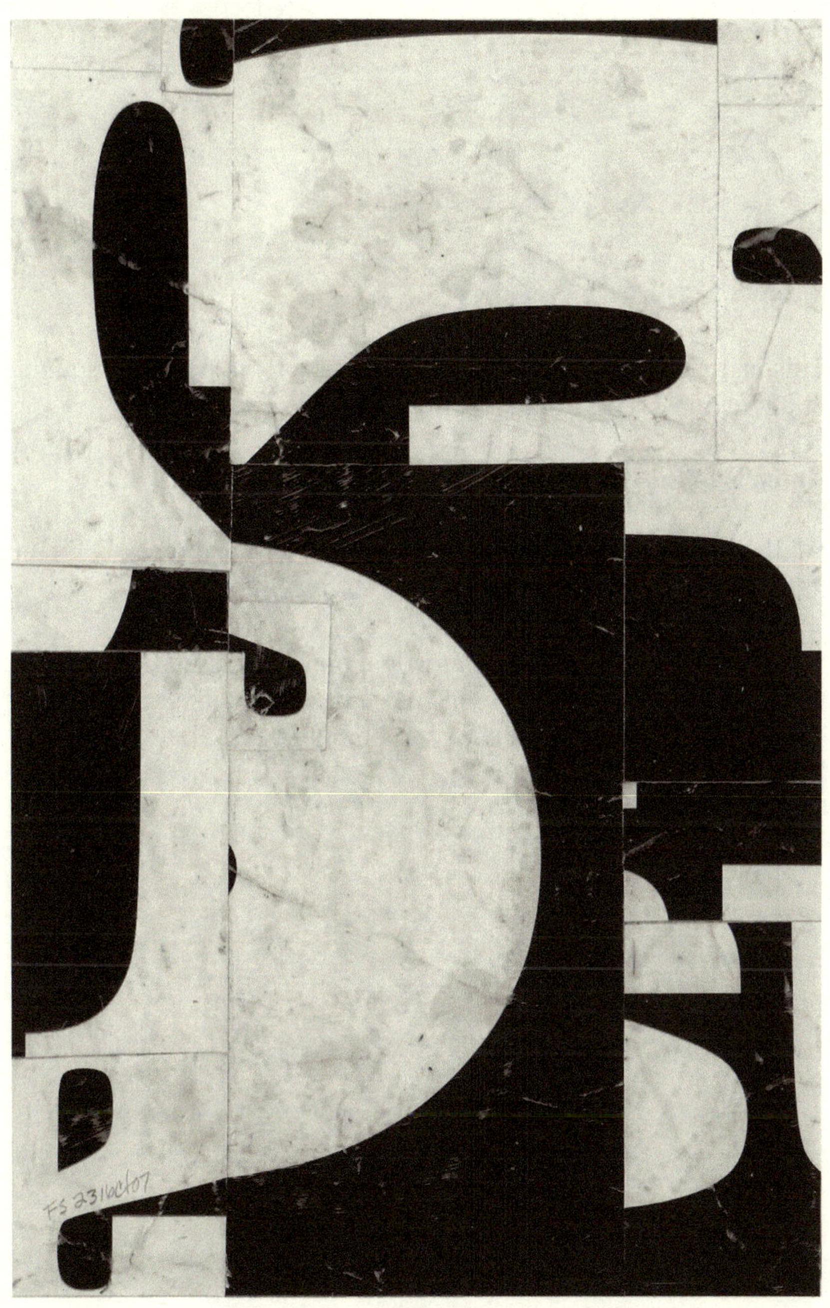

Plate 16

16

Monty Cantsin's Commentary:

This is not a plate of smoked ruby-red fatty pork nor baby squid in its own ink. This is not a paintbrush. It is a new day.

Karen Eliot's Commentary

While in Paris I go out for a walk, I shop. This is the biggest thing to avoid of course. So I merely browse.

Successful philosophizing is mostly a matter of circumlocuting thought. You talk around things more than you talk about things. This is the only way for a neoist to hit his target. That's very French.

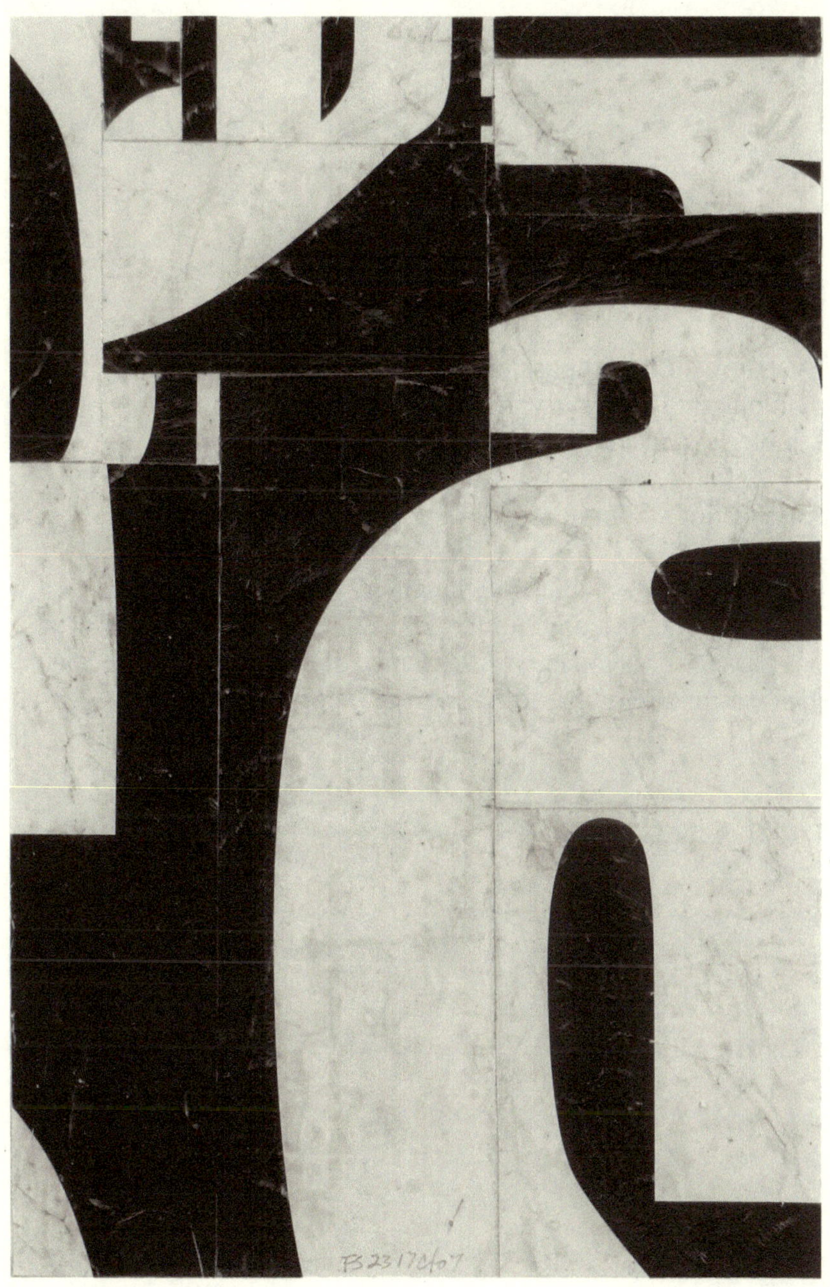

Plate 17

17

Monty Cantsin's Commentary:

Even now, it is still possible to actively engage in Neoism, by manipulating its history, here, in the present.
I think the constant rethinking of Neoism is important.

Karen Eliot's Commentary

Can the academy recuperate laughter?
"Art no longer has anything to say, if it ever did." A lot of what has passed for Neoism was flatulence of a different snort. This idea was and remains, some form of rapprochement.

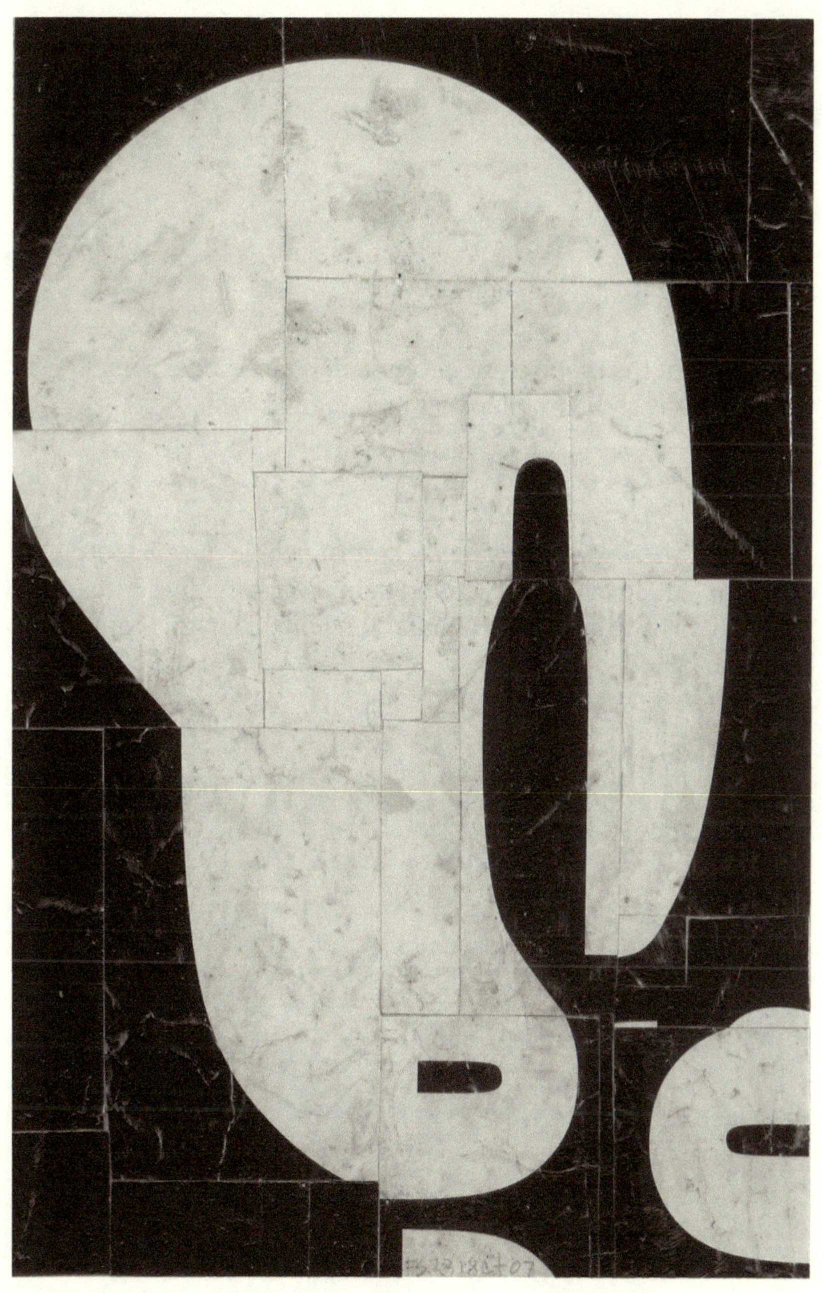

Plate 18

18

Monty Cantsin's Commentary:

Neoists want to escape from the "prison of art" and change the world or at least their underwear on a regular basis.

Karen Eliot's Commentary

The third criteria of Neoism leaves most people puzzled, especially the employees of the cultural apparatus.
This can only be taken as a sign of just how taboo this form of language is.

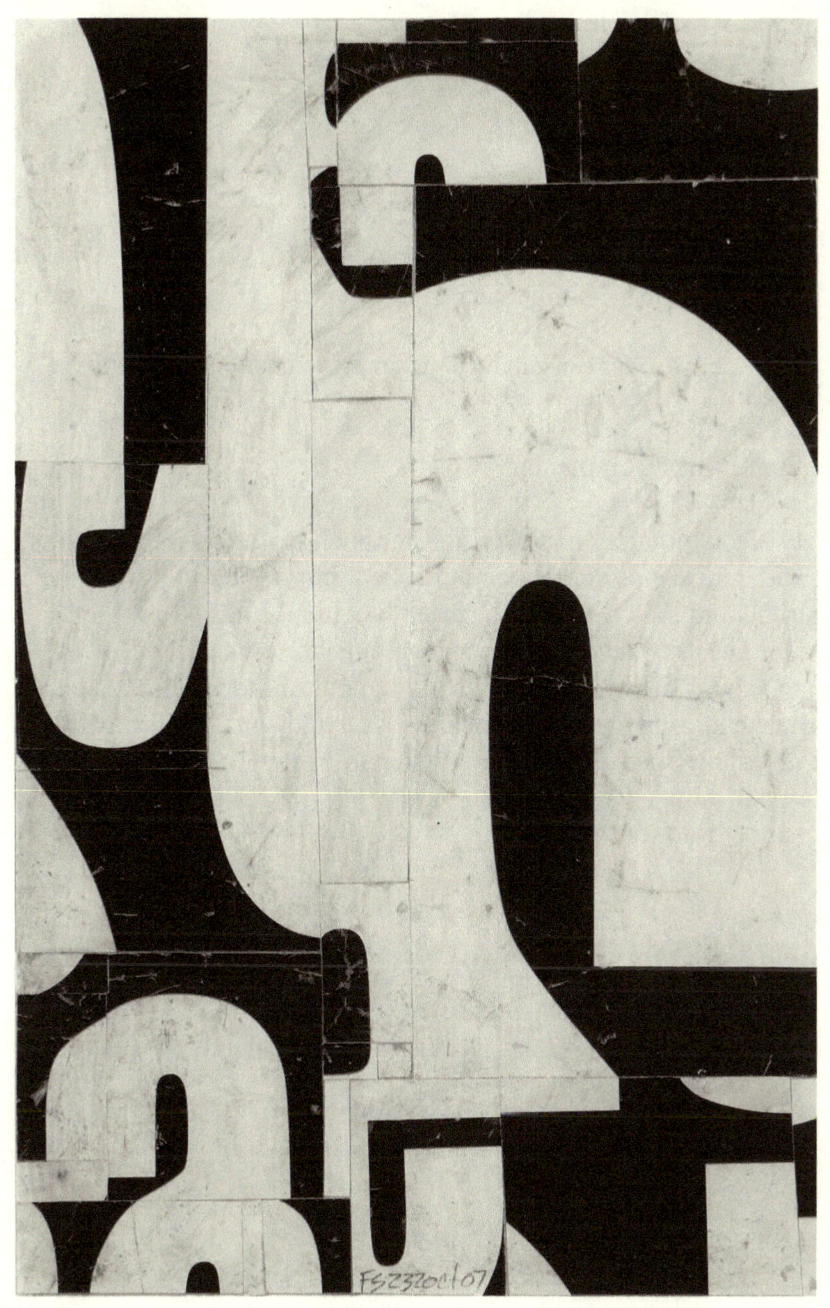

Plate 19

19

Monty Cantsin's Commentary:

The lack of need for censorship is the improvement of the practice of Neoism.

Karen Eliot's Commentary

My Neoist journey had acquired so much historical baggage that I had to hire a porter. When I checked into a hotel in Berlin, the girl behind the counter just started laughing. I had to ask the other guests to move their baggage outside so that all of my baggage could fit in the lobby. I soon ran out of money for tips and, at the end of my stay, had a garage sale and sold or gave away everything I had acquired. I now regard myself as being a master.

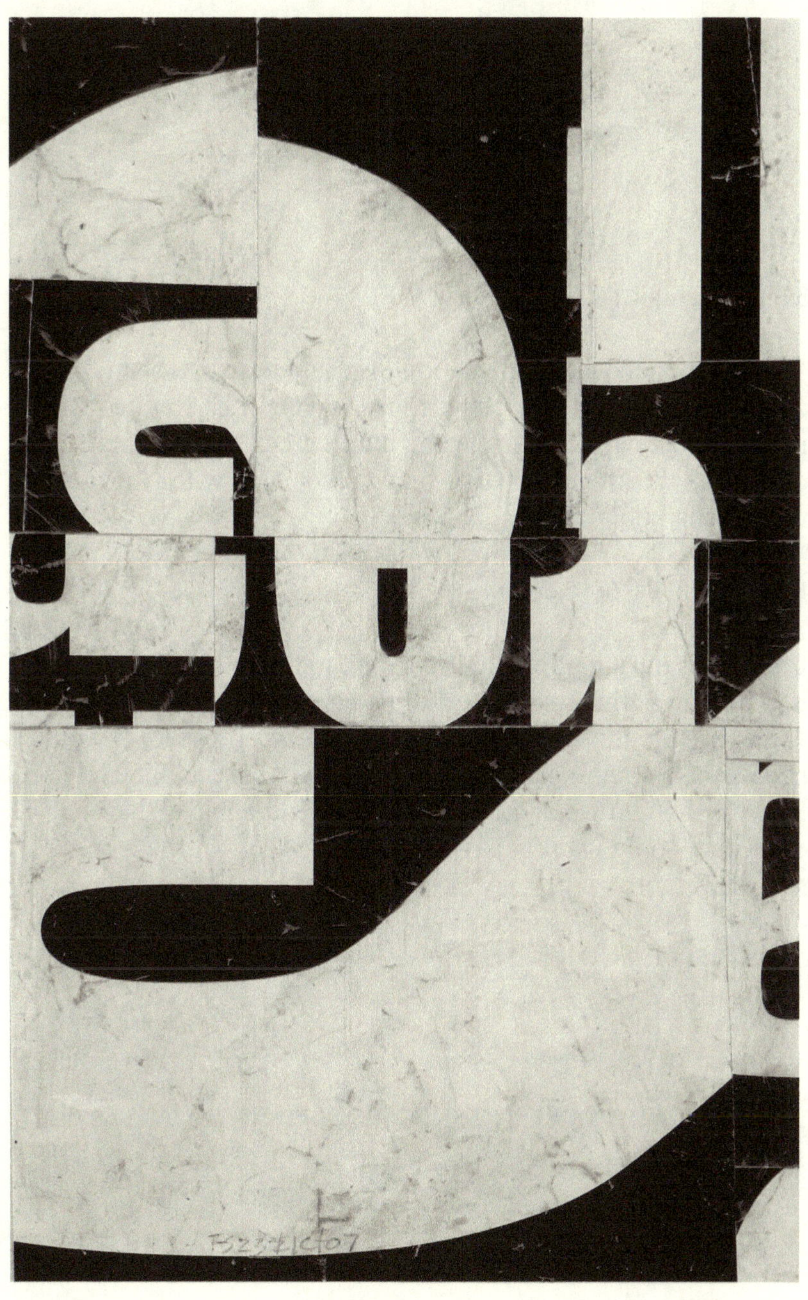

Plate 20

Monty Cantsin's Commentary:

There is no adequate explanation of what caused Neoism. I can assure you all, in no way, shape, or form can I be credited with its invention. My conscience and hands are clean. The main characters we often hear of as being associated with Neoism are merely shameful poseurs.

Karen Eliot's Commentary

Capitalists must be flexible if they are to exploit Neoism for all it is worth. Perhaps some sort of neoist surcharge or a constantly depleting privatized neoist product could be proposed. It would need to be something as successful as digital space, time, electricity or bottled water that creates an unending need that everyone would happily pay a monthly fee for. Perhaps some sort of widget.

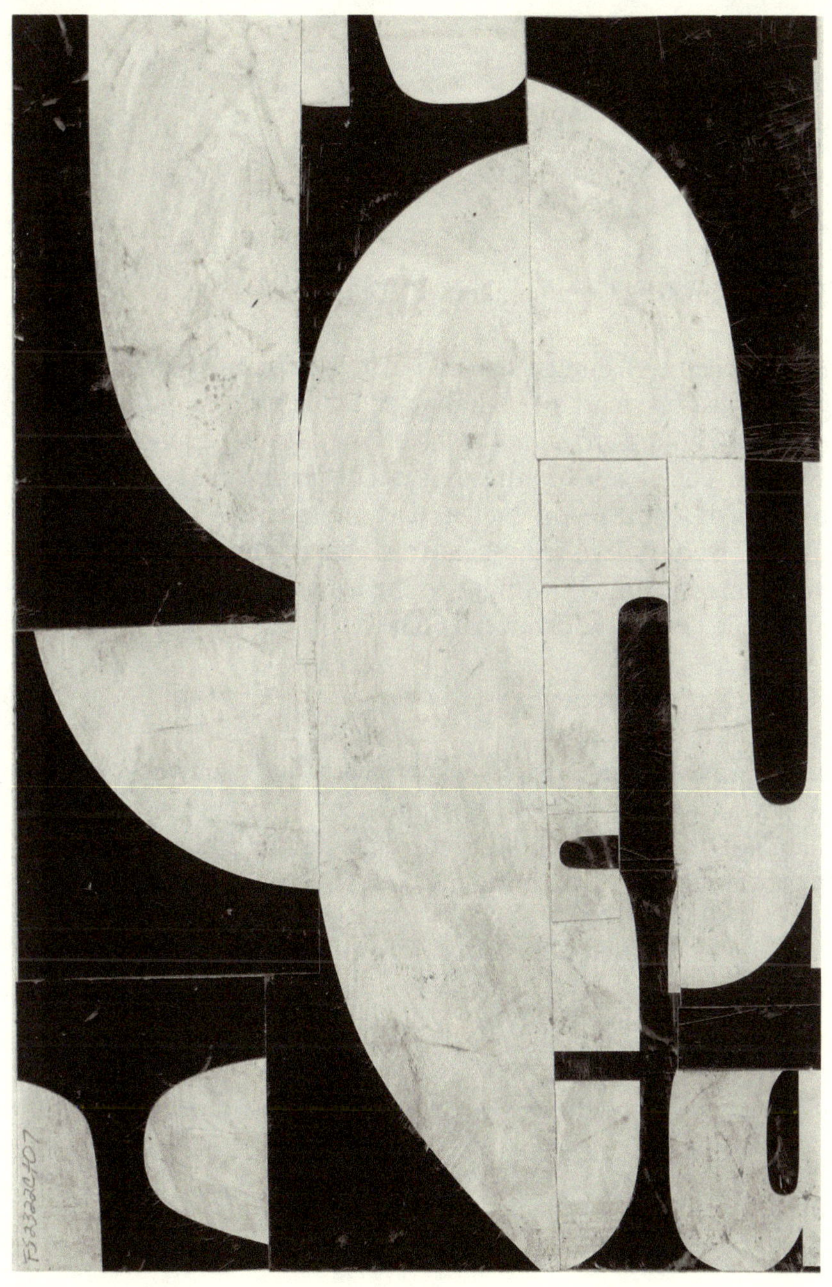

Plate 21

21

Monty Cantsin's Commentary:

In the scheme of things Neoism is often considered insignificant. This is just one mark of its failure and its poorly supported claims of failure are numerous. Neoism does not equal all Neoists. The Neoist Manifesto is not disinformation spread by all Neoists. Most fear it even as they applaud it. None of this is simple. Neoism IS a mind-game and that might explain this whole mess perfectly without, in the least, dispelling any confusion. It is best if quoted out of context.

Karen Eliot's Commentary

If it were true that 'girls just want to have fun' then we would not waste our time on Neoists. What a bunch of losers they are! And I am not one of them contrary to whatever that filthy Monty has to say about me. Don't bring me down today.

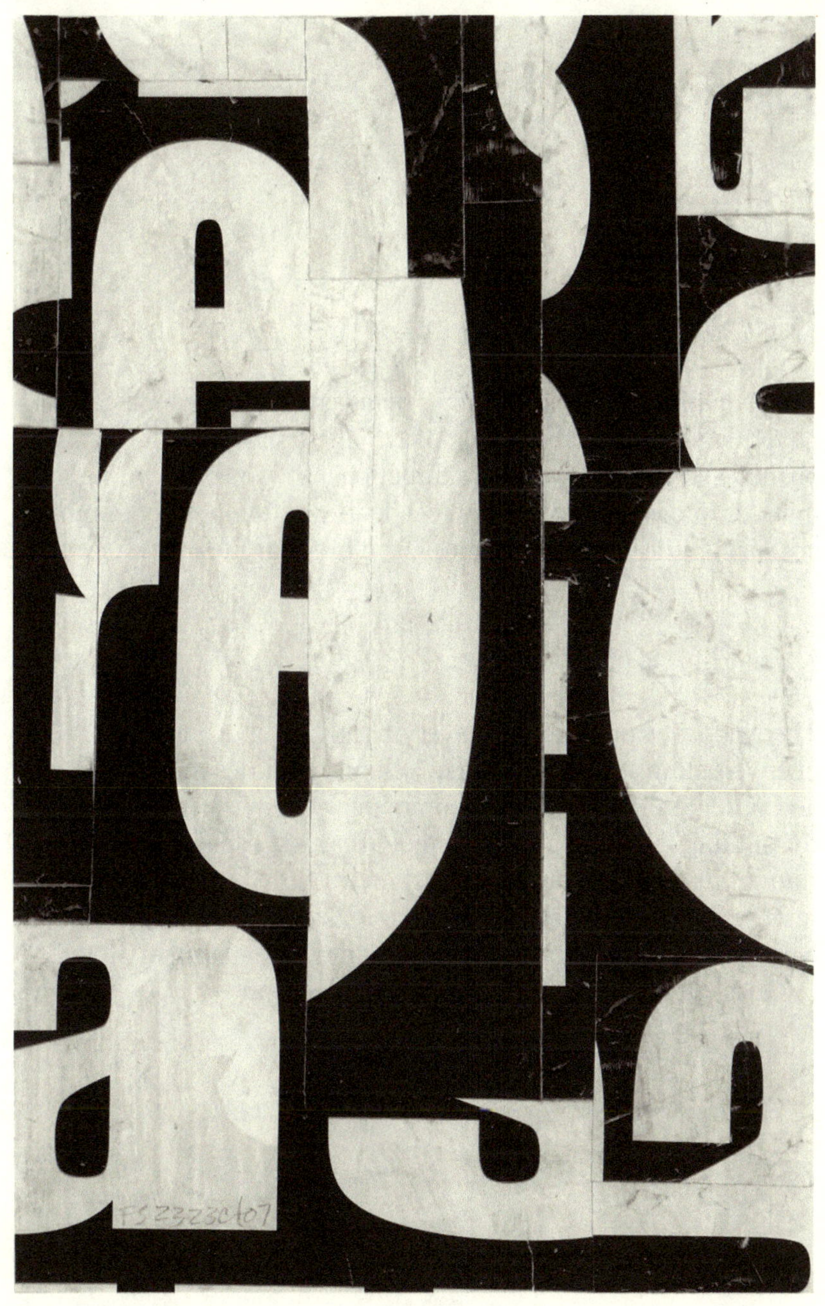

Plate 22

Monty Cantsin's Commentary:

Touchon himself has a smoothly persuasive voice which can still hover deliciously on the verge of ecstatic breakthrough. We are pushed and shoved in endless directions. It would be wrong to think or quote the expected antecedents or attempt to pre-empt criticisms. That would seem to leave time for little else.

Karen Eliot's Commentary

The Neoists want to recycle everything. We take our fun seriously creating serious art works a thousand times more profound and obscure than any critic's commentary about them. It is not for nothing that many Neoists, including and especially artists, find it impossible as they endlessly reinvent what they are and represent. The question of audience really is not an issue. Most Neoist masters are happy to work in complete obscurity, forsaking even an affiliation with the field of Neoism.

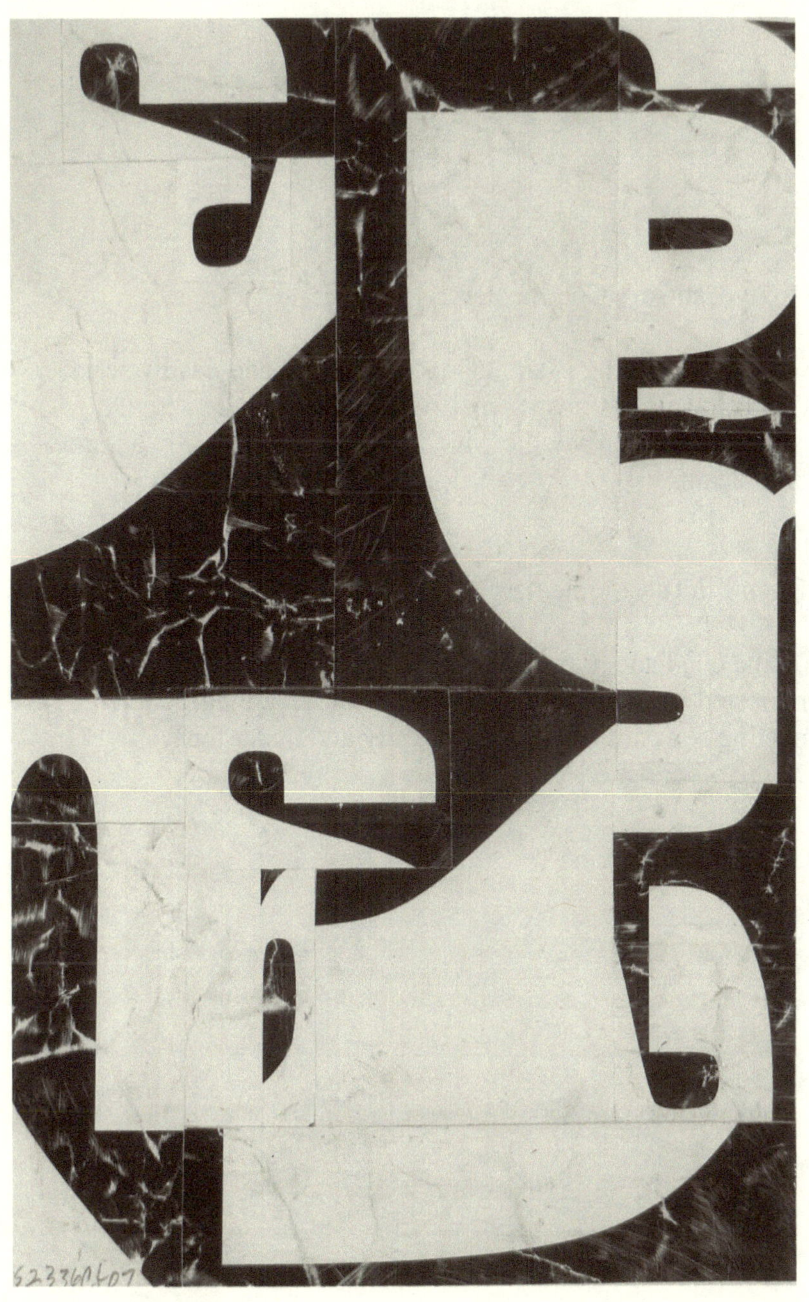

Plate 23

23

Monty Cantsin's Commentary:

Self-understanding is simultaneously ironic and deadly serious. This is the almost unspoken aspect of avant-garde activity; to ridicule and destroy logic which is seen as a clinically administered death.

Karen Eliot's Commentary

On the one hand, the theorizing of critics who weren't so much interested in addressing the status of art in capitalist societies, as meeting sex partners who were 'dirty and under thirty'.
On the other hand...

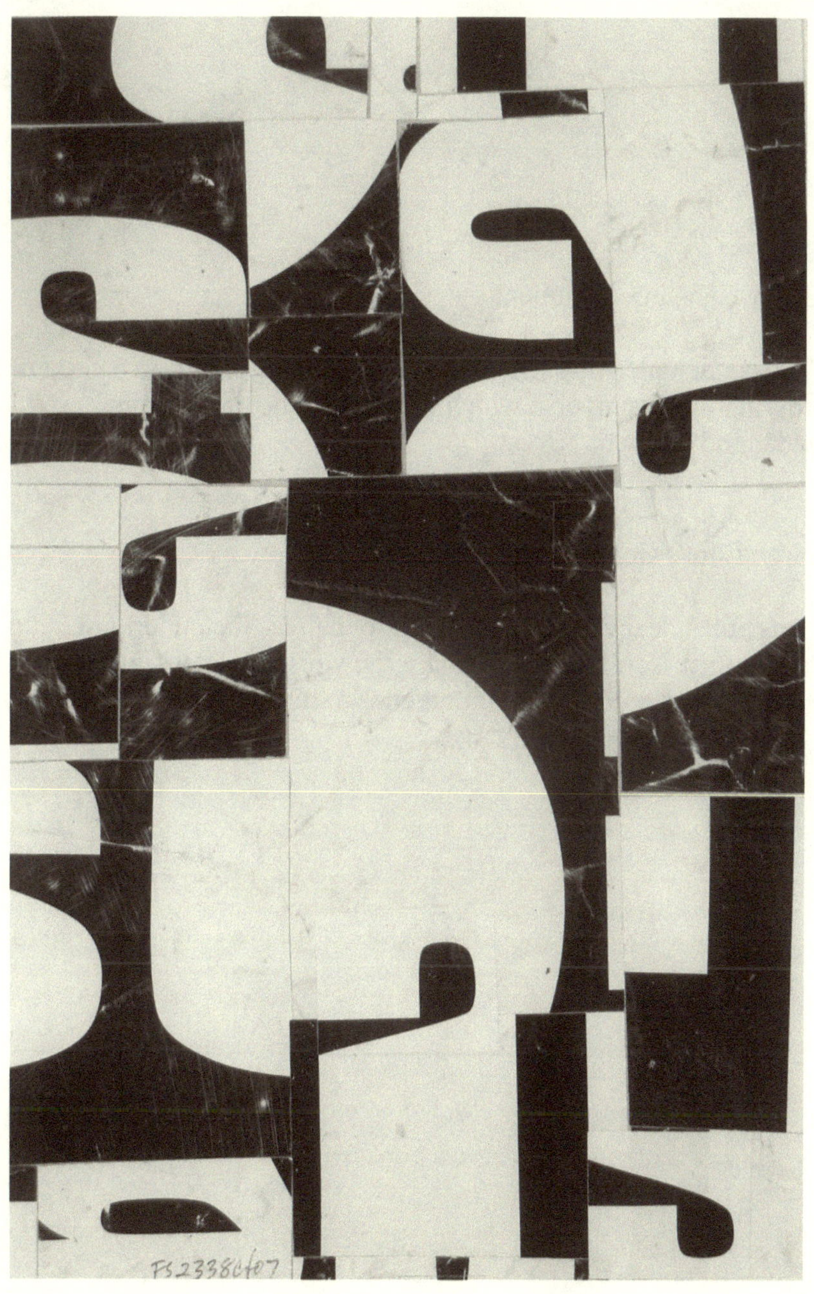

Plate 24

Monty Cantsin's Commentary:

Transcendental, self-sufficient - I prefer to think of it as a certain ordering of the universe which is the attribute of a spiritual leader and of every Neoist.

Karen Eliot's Commentary

Texts are a clear example of trying to express the underlying marginality. Neoists seek to warm the world by attaching chaotic elements to it. Guiding their audience to do the same, they try to evoke its hidden faculties.

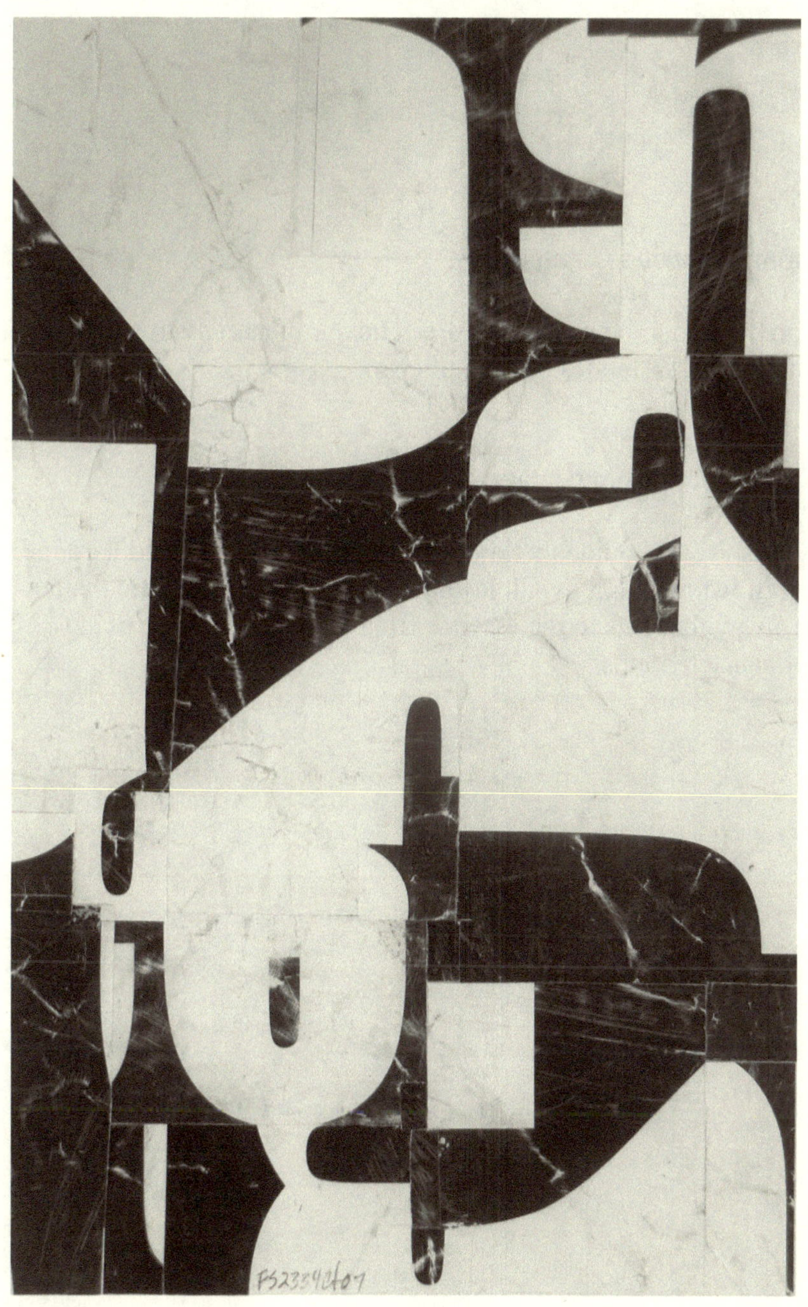

Plate 25

25

Monty Cantsin's Commentary:

Too evident to be neglected: dialectical immaterialism with the totalitarian aesthetics of romanticism.

Karen Eliot's Commentary

To inspire and guide the liberation - a cooling down and hardening of warm, fluid, dynamic spirit to cold, hard and static matter in a way that gets to the essence from which no residue of significance remains.

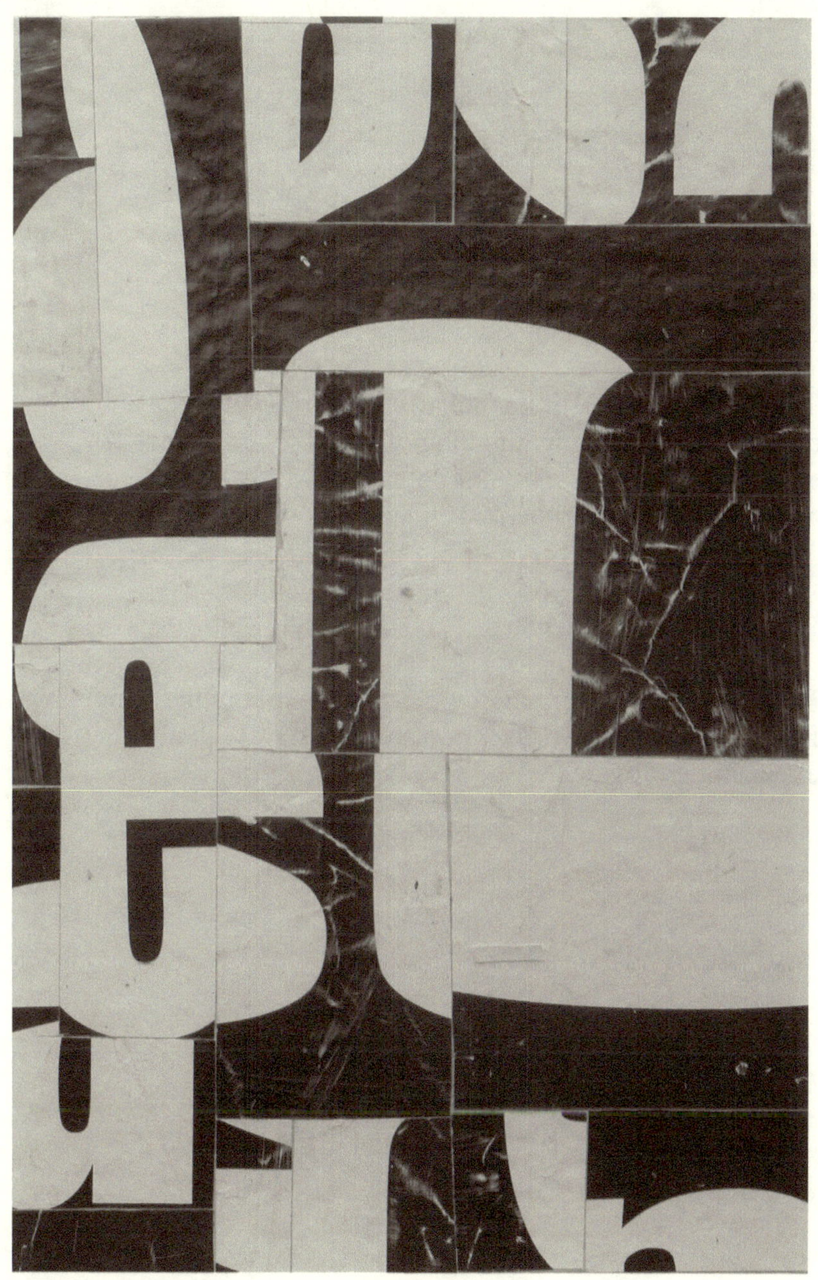

Plate 26

26

Monty Cantsin's Commentary:

The mind must substitute the quest for words with the abbreviated bits of lettering by thinking of their broken sounds & recognizing them as the same sounds of words - if you can find any. This is an experiment in expanding consciousness.

Karen Eliot's Commentary

Plow up raw, fresh ground by breathing into it rather than blowing onto it. Creatively takes control over how with no explanation provided.

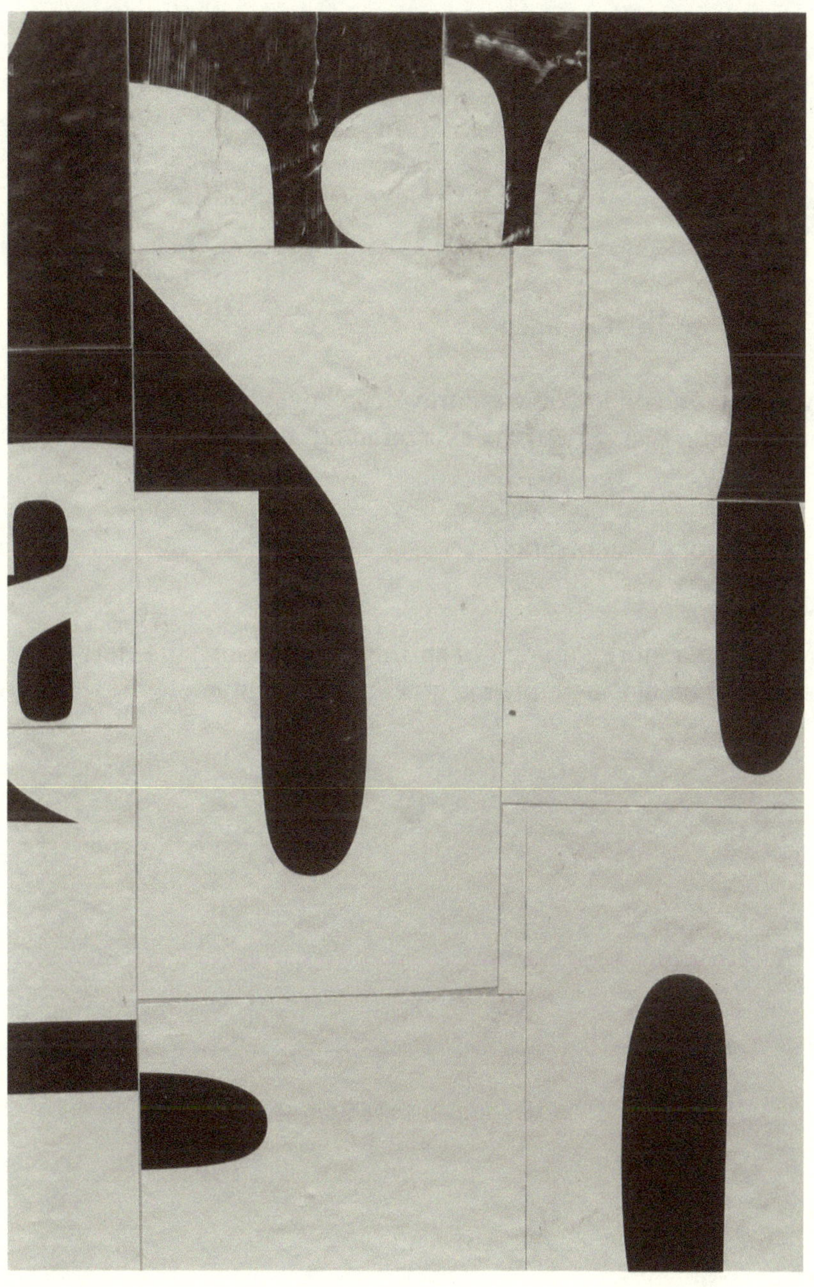

Plate 27

27

Monty Cantsin's Commentary:

A sort of beacon to wayward travelers, engaging them enough to put them on that path of the exception not the rule.

Karen Eliot's Commentary

Words are a murky morass of shifting, competing signifiers of tragic impotence, a grapheme gruel in midnight hues.

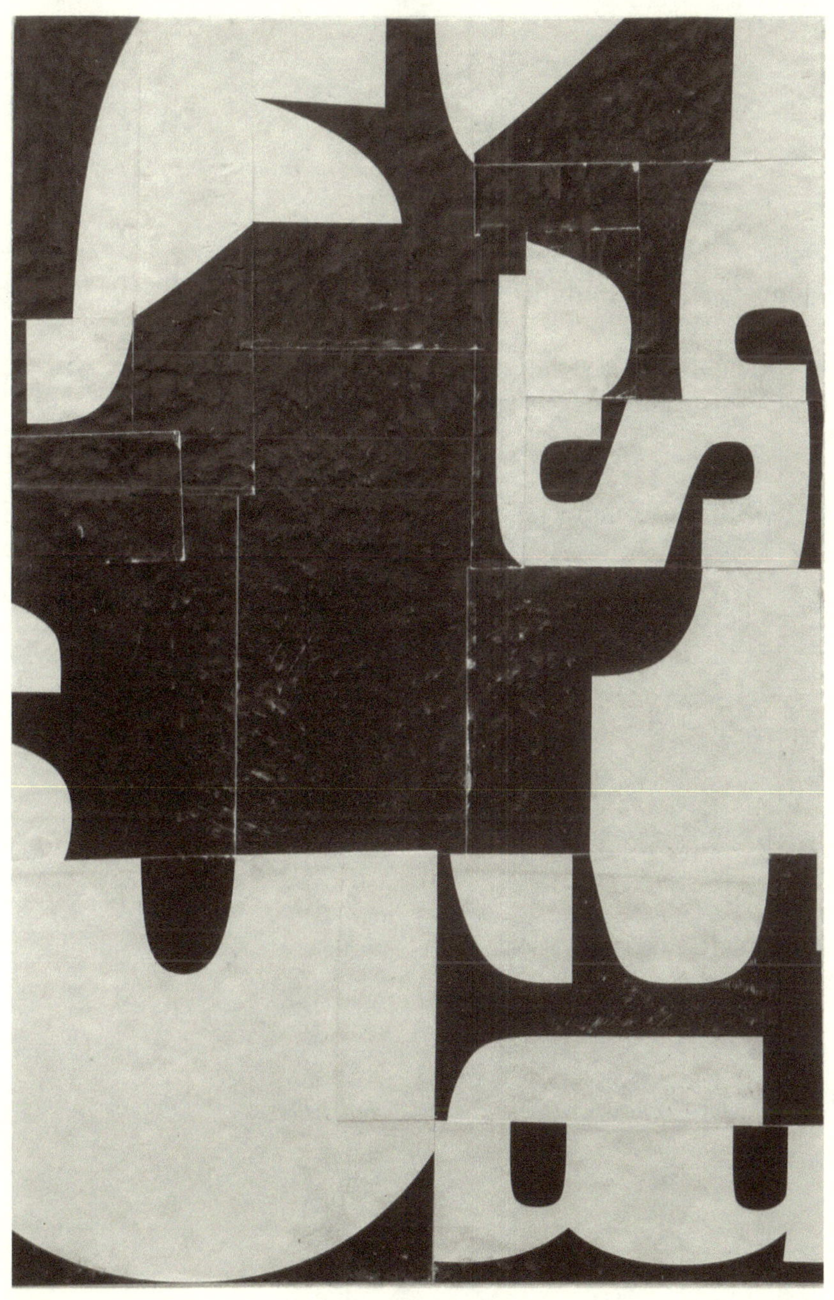

Plate 28

28

Monty Cantsin's Commentary:

A critical theory attacking wishful thinking about freedom with never a whisper in terms of old-hat artistic ideas.

Karen Eliot's Commentary

A red herring - the only fish we’re frying.

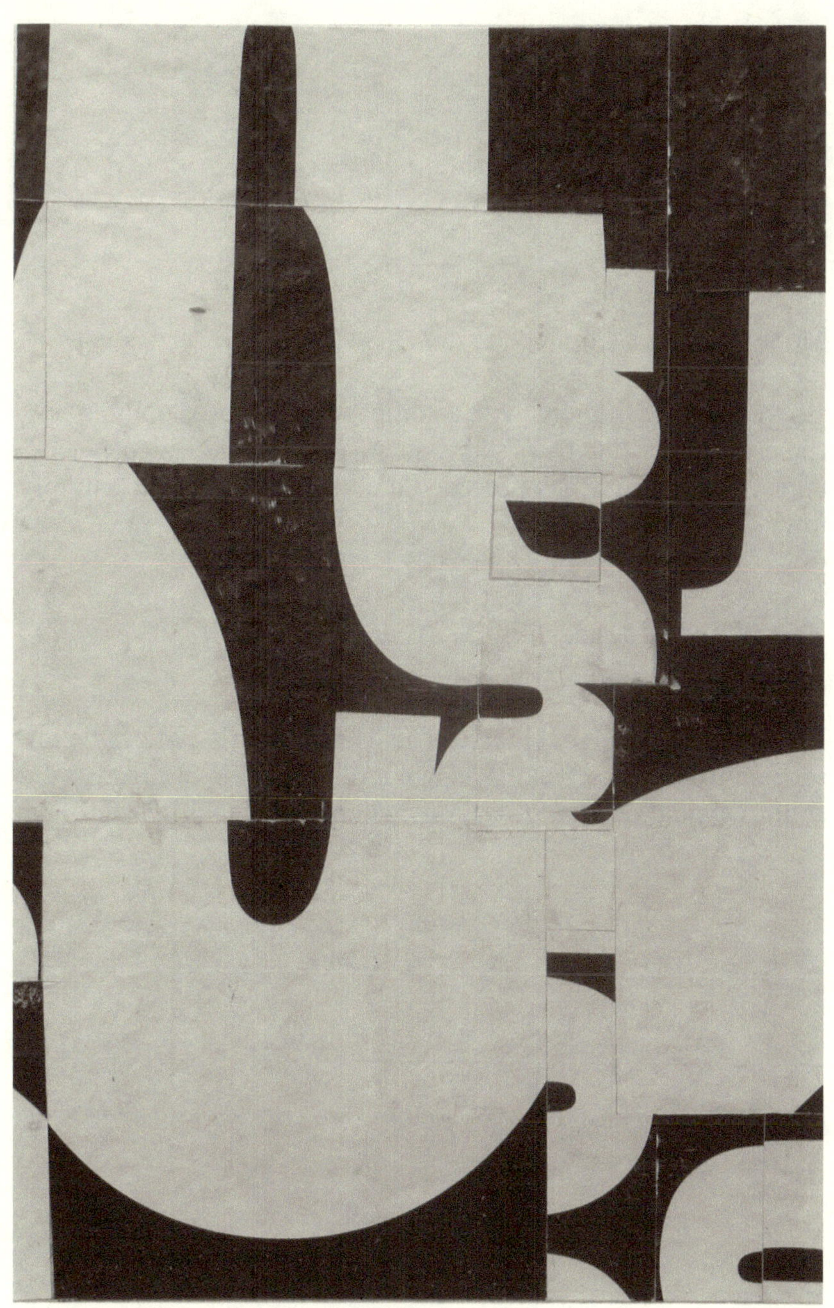

Plate 29

29

Monty Cantsin's Commentary:

Go through the motions with a smile, strive towards nothing because nothing is the truly stable state. What we do is dependent upon the nothing which preceded it and the nothing that will follow.

Karen Eliot's Commentary

The Neoists are ungovernable. This is particularly noticeable in relation to the texts. Text is an agent of control. Word for word, actions should be humorous in which total subjectivity rules.

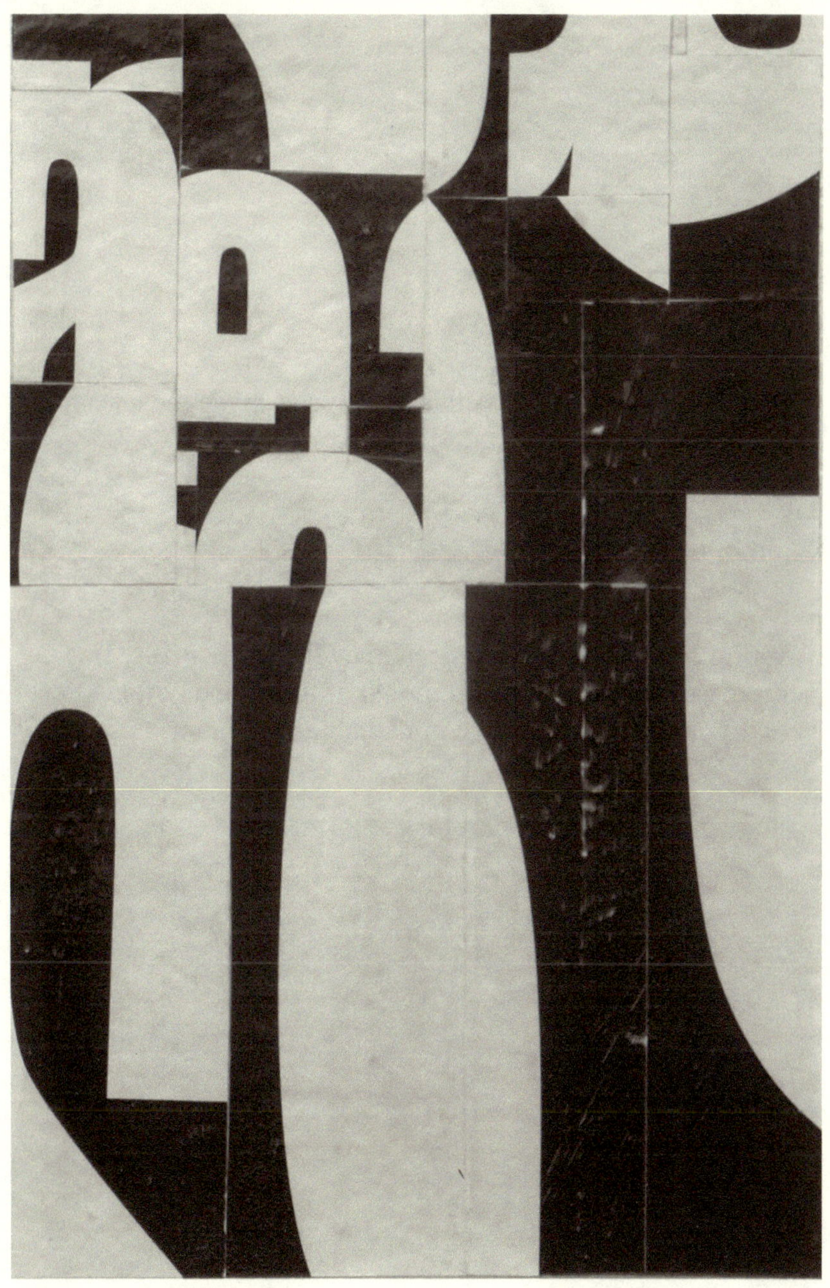

Plate 30

Monty Cantsin's Commentary:

Telephones and telephone bells have always made me uneasy and raise some interesting questions in philosophy!

Karen Eliot's Commentary

Hovering over all the jabbering and pewling, personality fragments dissolve, the self-muted mouth of the divine - afterwards, there is nothing left knowable or ownable.

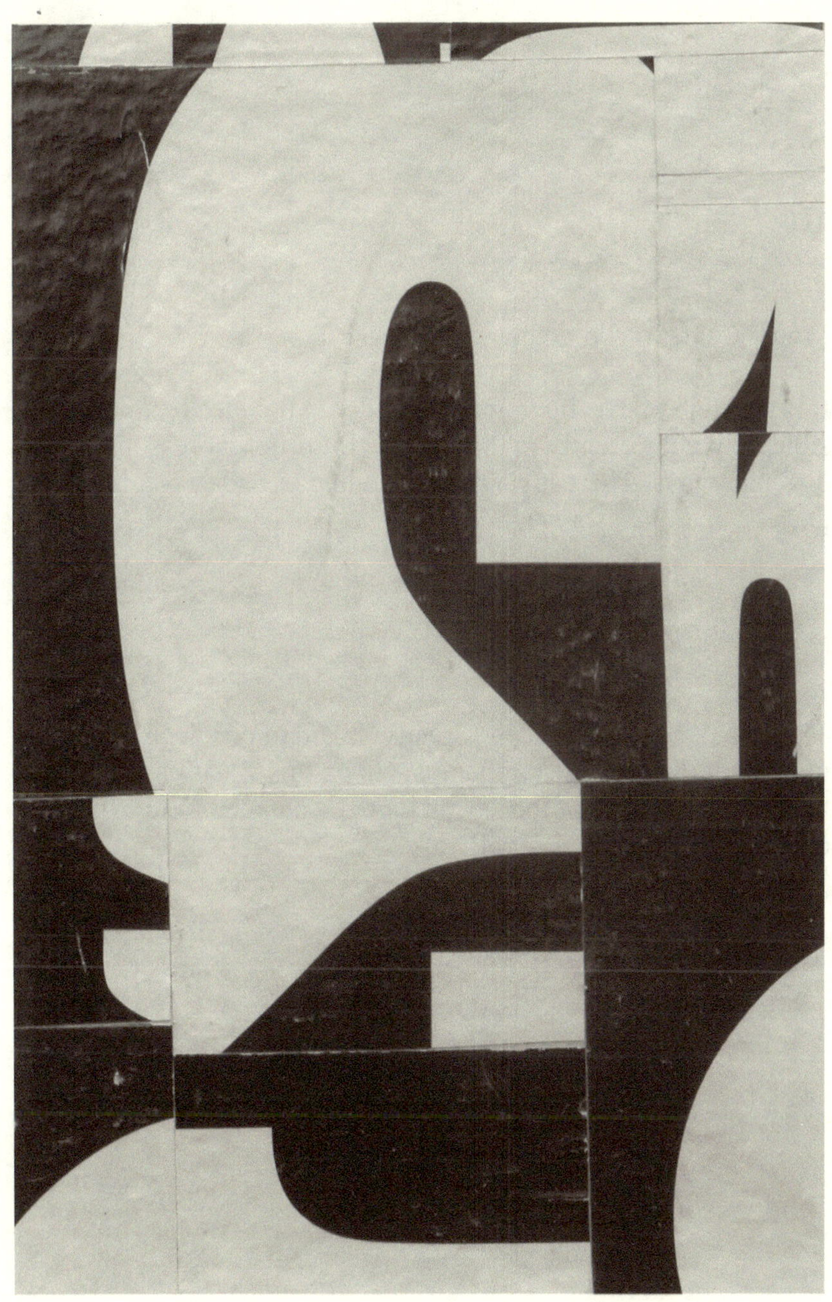

Plate 31

31

Monty Cantsin's Commentary:

It is possible to overflow unrestrainedly in the idea that it is possible to live differently in this world, for different reasons and in different ways. There is no real beginning or end to Neoism, it goes on and on… forever…

Karen Eliot's Commentary

The idea of the "original" is directly linked to privilege thereby upholding the very idea of genius. Given this situation, do we lament the collapse of the "avant garde" - an attempt to expose and explode, once and for all?

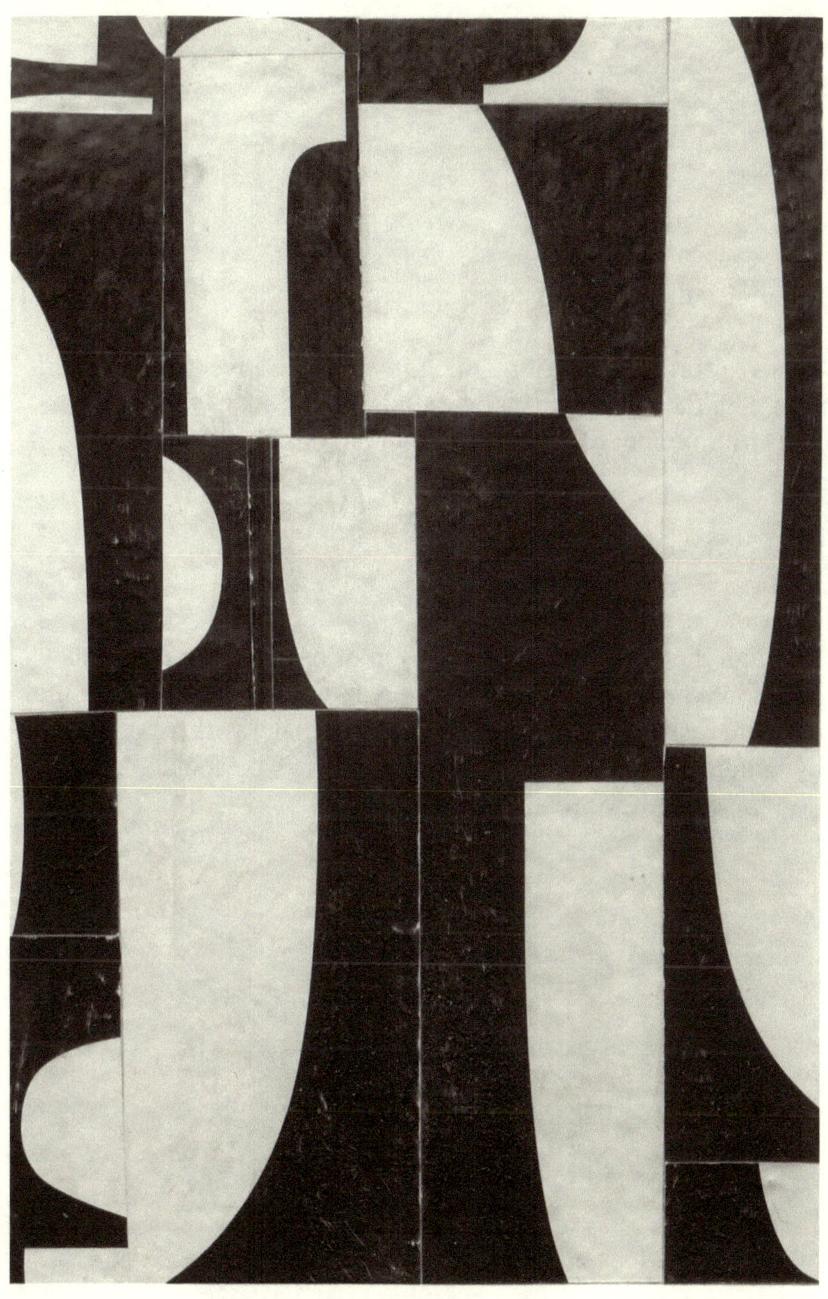

Plate 32

32

Monty Cantsin's Commentary:

This is a form of negation which involves re-inventing those who would control us as a potential revolutionary force - a perfect environment for an underground to develop.

Karen Eliot's Commentary

Through the conscious manipulation of pre-existing elements individual genius is embedded deep in our consciousness as the ultimate justification of private property. The world is populated by hundreds of millions of geniuses. There's no social justification for what they are doing.

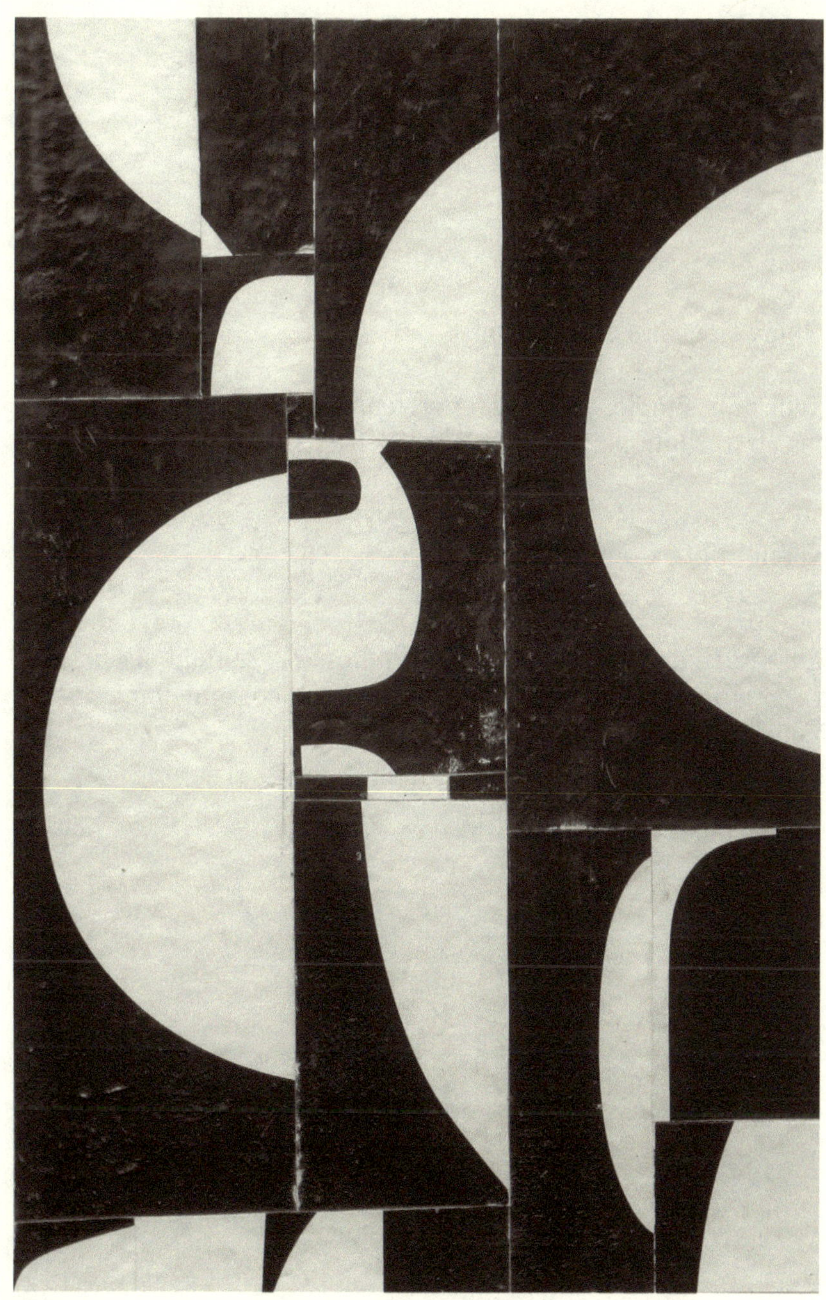

Plate 33

33

Monty Cantsin's Commentary:

Neoism is simple, amusing, unpretentious, requires no skill, and has no institutional value. It is the slacker's perfect art form.

Karen Eliot's Commentary

A transcendental idealism, a blue endless sky, a fluid discharge, a continuous moving on, a gesture of defiance, something unnamable.

Plate 34

34

Monty Cantsin's Commentary:

Neoism largely depends upon the true and living equality we will give up everything for.

Karen Eliot's Commentary

Within this society there is a general drift away from the over-identification by certain individuals with the context of Neoism.

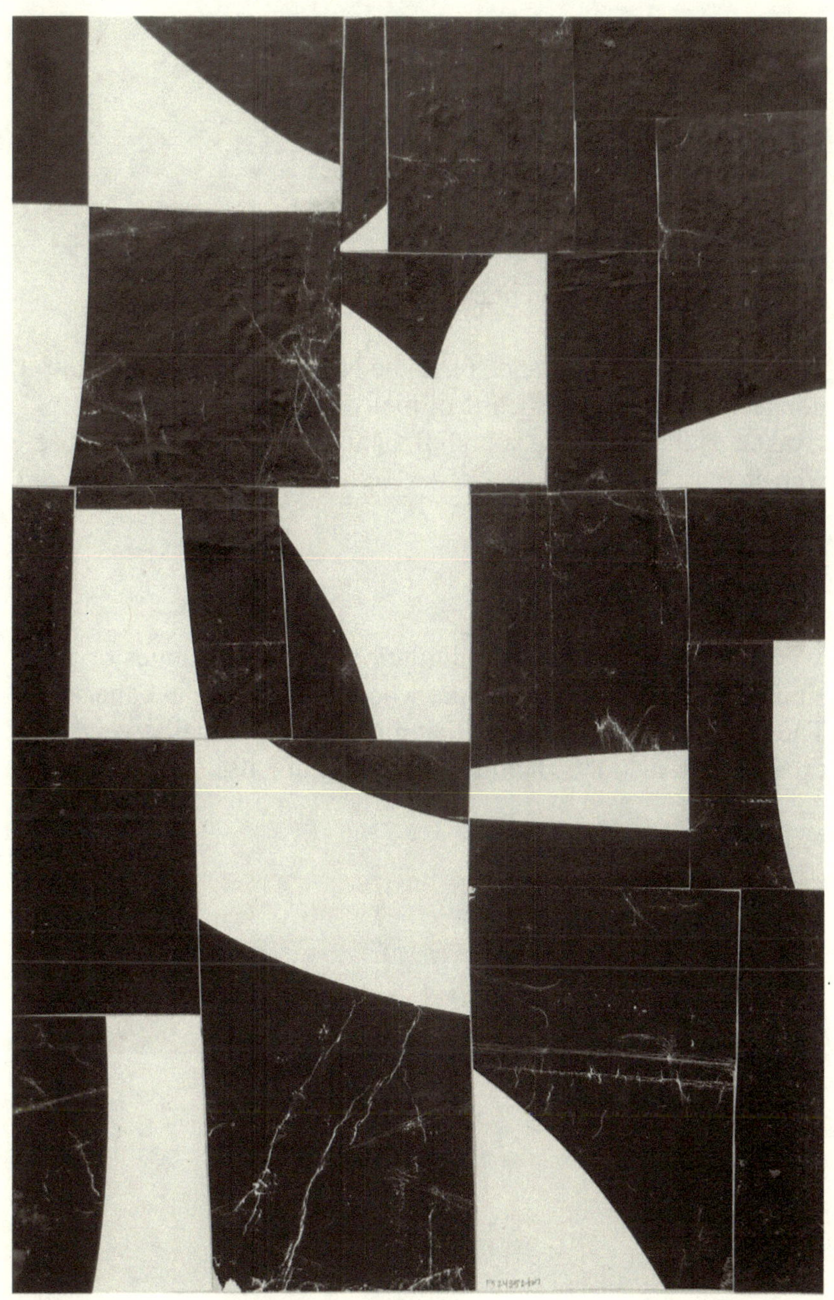

Plate 35

35

Monty Cantsin's Commentary:

In terms of both letter and spirit, the Neoists have sown agitation and disquiet in the hearts of many. It is in the effort to awaken as the annoying sound of an alarm clock awakens those who sleep.

Karen Eliot's Commentary

We are very touchy about assimilation and the dynamics of assimilation. This leaves aside the whole issue of social cohesion. The “getting a job” rationale that most live by actually weighs on them and distracts them from Neoist pursuits.

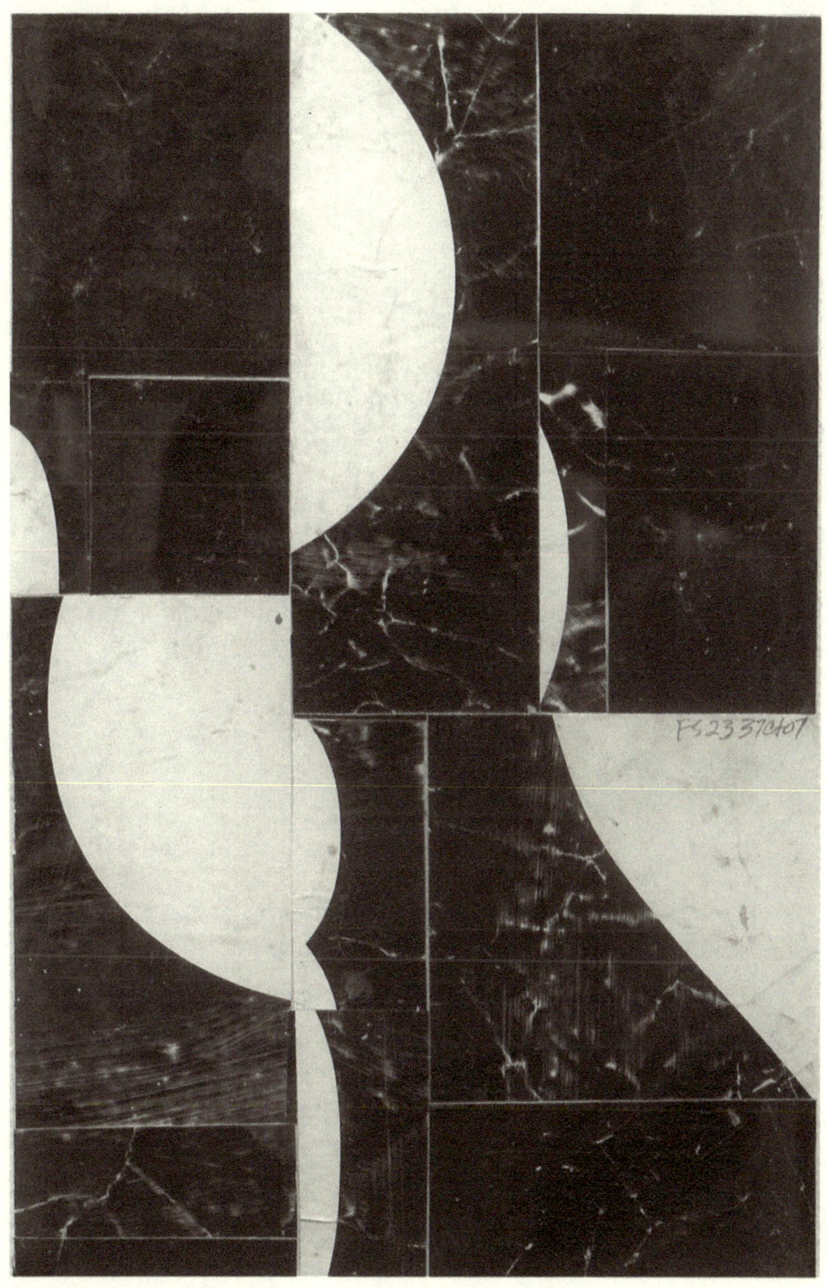

Plate 36

36

Monty Cantsin's Commentary:

To undergo a radical - and more importantly, permanent - transformation takes considerable time and effort

Karen Eliot's Commentary

Water from the rock, manna and the quail, this whole affair is wholly dependent on the Neoist's persistent attention.

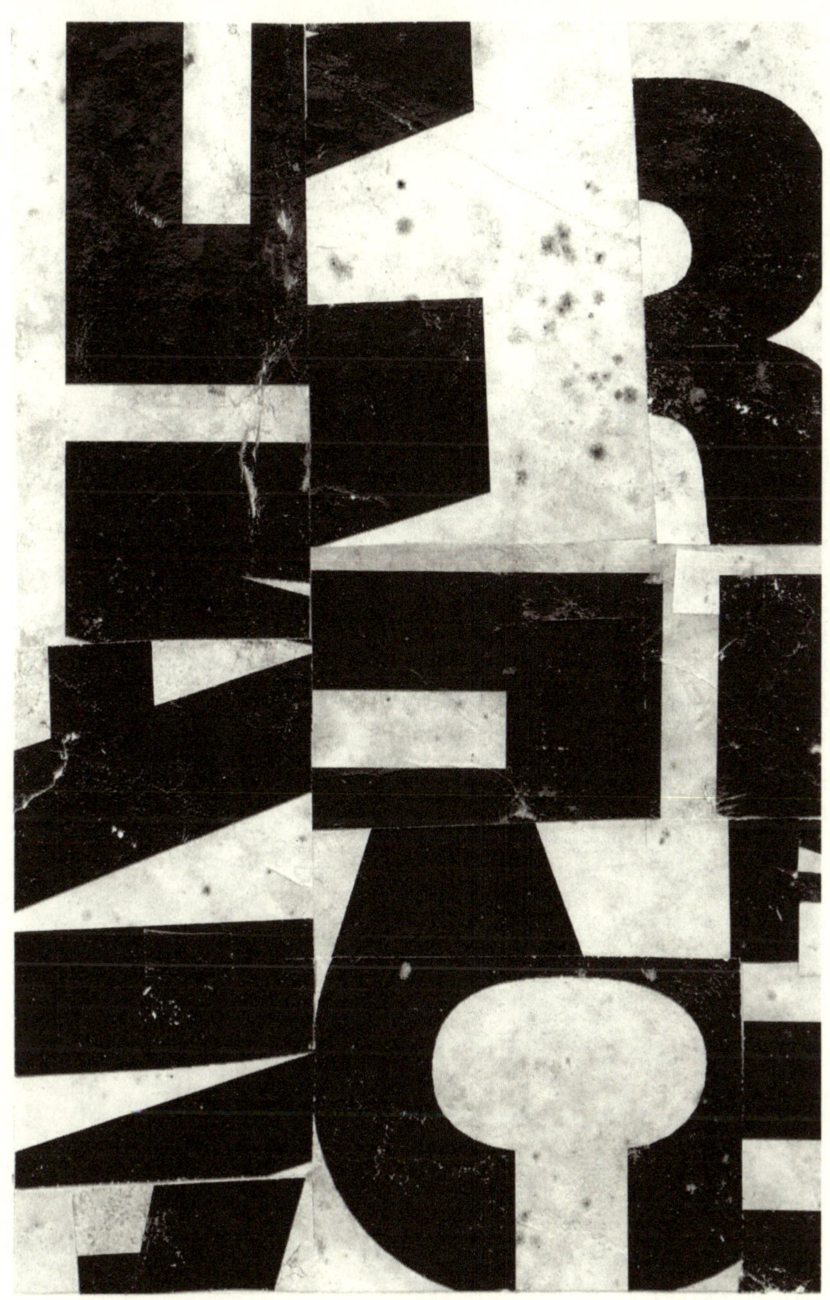

Plate 37

37

Monty Cantsin's Commentary:

There is abundant empirical evidence that Neoism is in the process of "going away" but then, also of “arriving”.

Karen Eliot's Commentary

It's actually good to have a couple of shocks to the paradigm now and again but not so often that numbness sets in. In the massive overdose of information brought on by the internet many people have moved from being shocked to being in shock. From my experience as a woman I'm not sure who is occupying who - there are no clean and absolute divisions – and because of that it seems a stupid hair to split at this point. After all, I am merely the sum of all those who claim to be me.

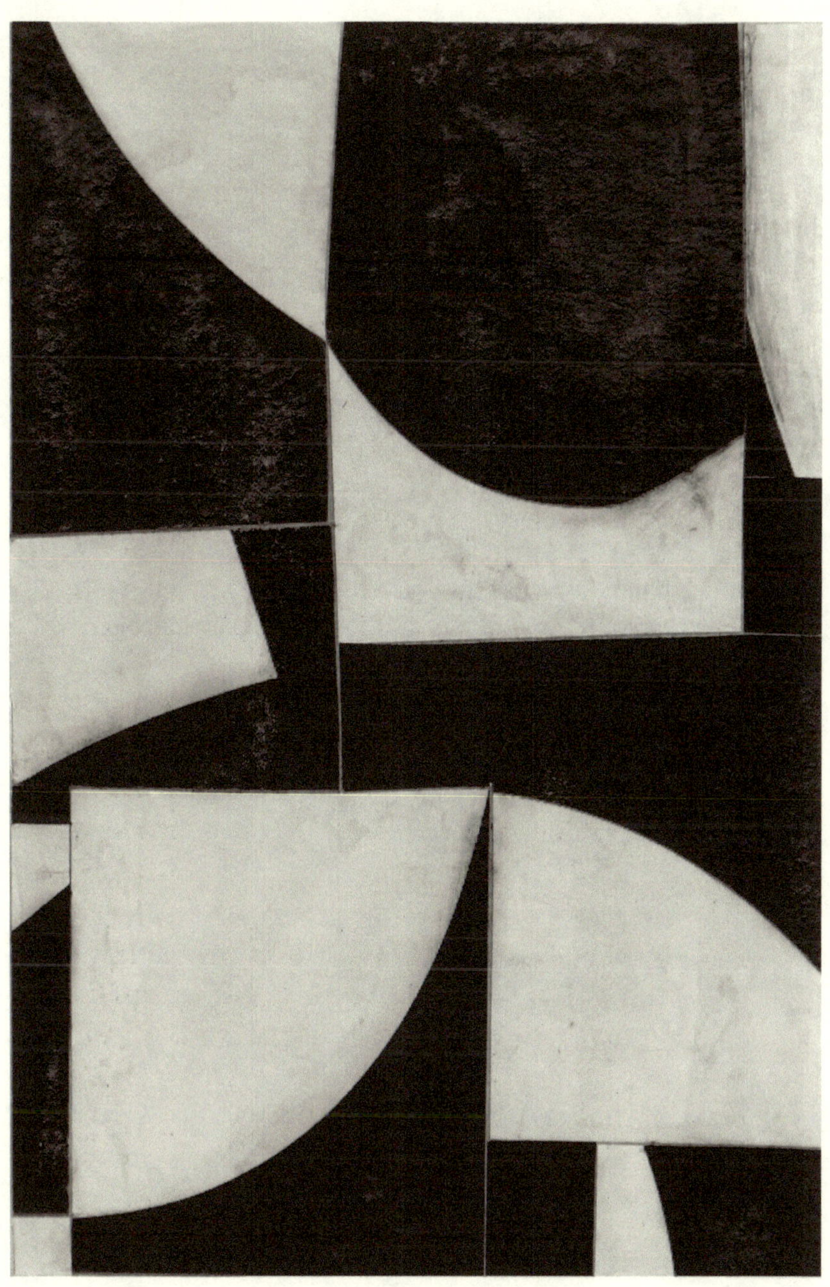

Plate 38

38

Monty Cantsin's Commentary:

Neoism needs to be protected, but so does the idea that once it has been undertaken, the work of the Neoist is truly the most important work we can do.

Karen Eliot's Commentary

Neoism is a balancing act that I have not mastered very well. The subtext of so many outsider groups in the past has been a desire to create a new insider position.

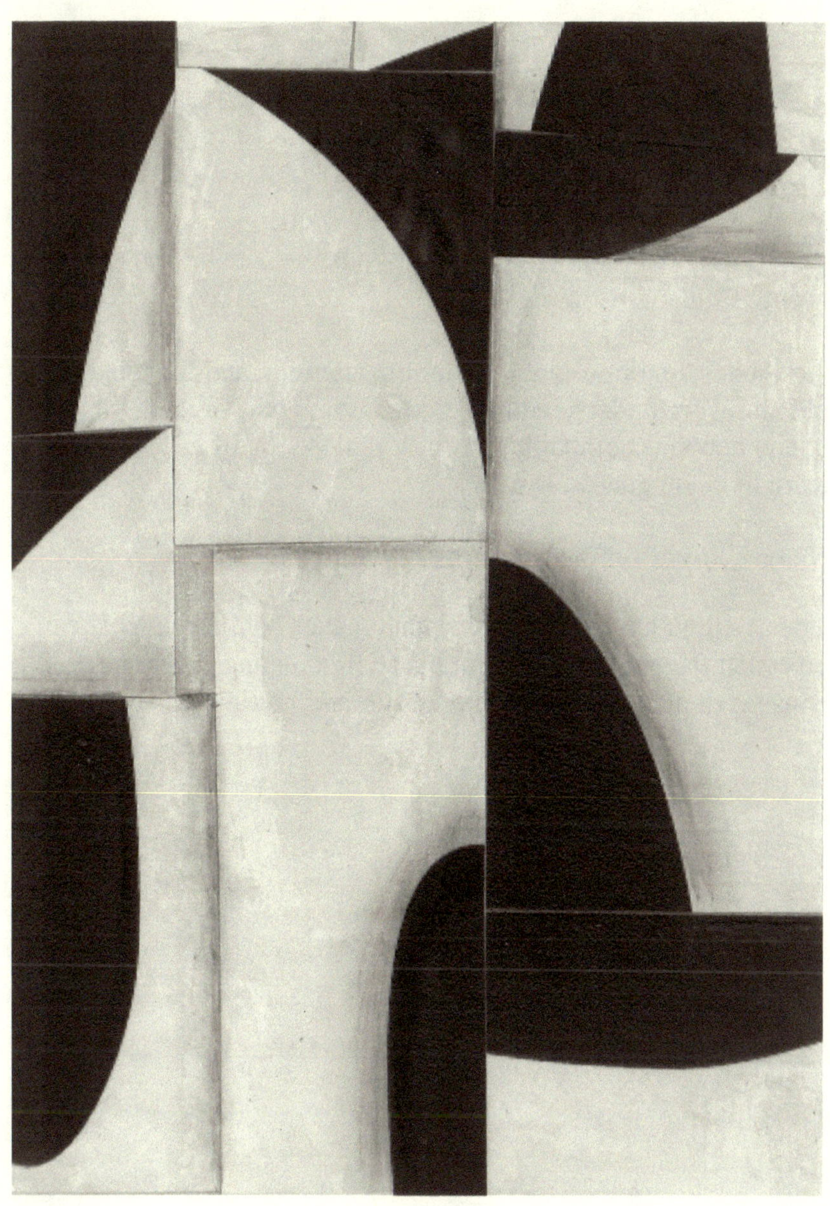

Plate 39

39

Monty Cantsin's Commentary:

Aesthetics are important in grabbing attention and for replacing old and worn understandings of self. Some will say that this phenomenon accompanies a robust philosophy of art. Neoists learn to be on guard for it.

Karen Eliot's Commentary

The desire to have contempt is what makes conflict in what can be called the uncultivated mind. The first untangling strategy consists of a debate between a lobster and boiling water.

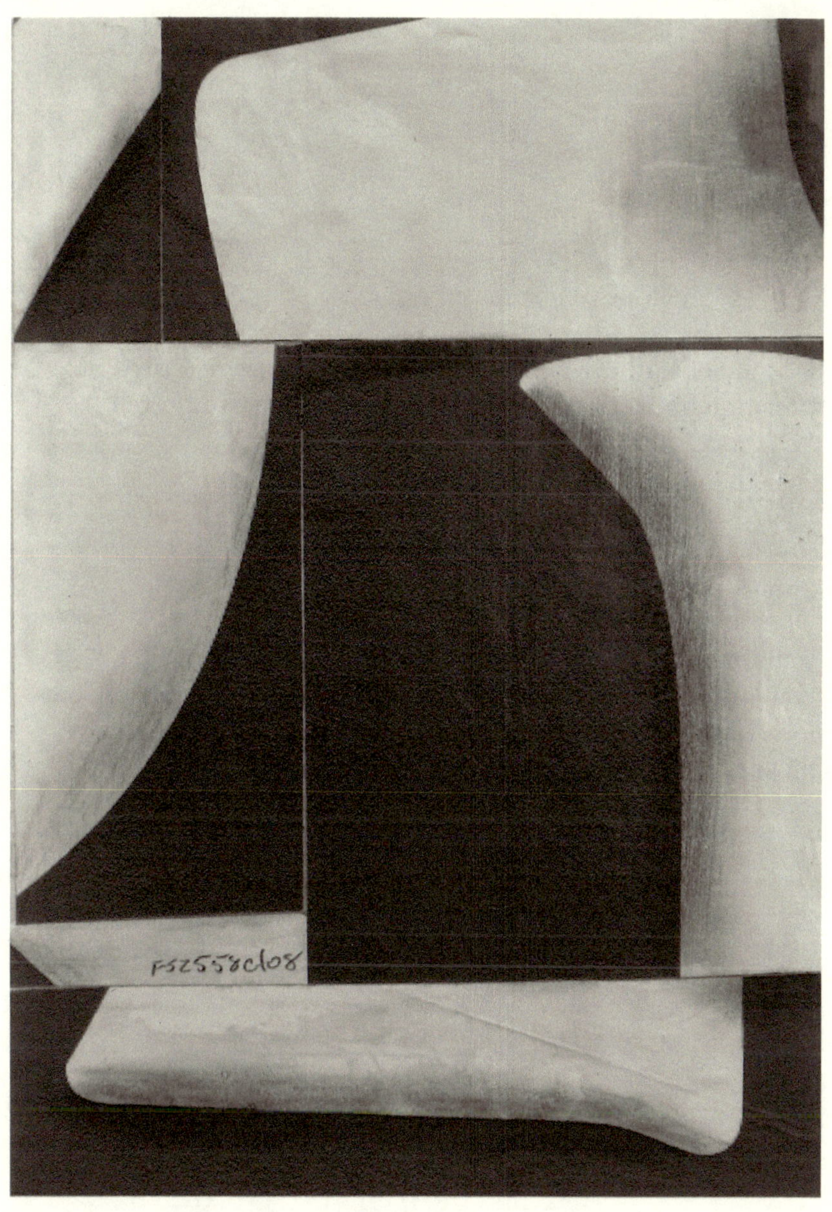

Plate 40

Monty Cantsin's Commentary:

The methods of reflective equilibrium that survive a robust examination of the concrete implications are achieved when divergence cannot be further reduced.

Karen Eliot's Commentary

With respect to poetic form an enormous amount of time is spent thinking to explain its relevance to the point under discussion. With that caution, there may still be some useful advice I can pass along. Well, not really. At least not this year.

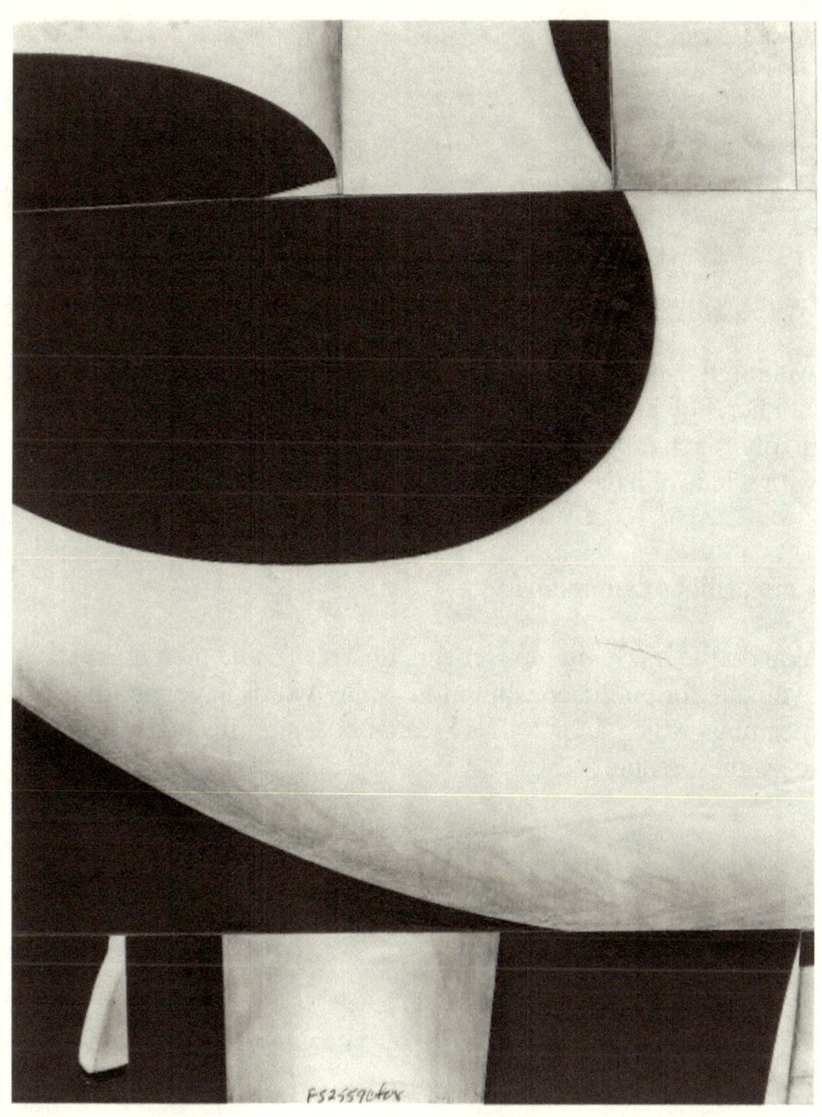

Plate 41

41

Monty Cantsin's Commentary:

Although there is no univocal understanding of the term, Neoism is inherently creative since it involves making numerous choices, involves actively rethinking history's uses and incorporates it with what we have been able to retrieve from the gutter.

Karen Eliot's Commentary

You don't simply dig up Neoism, dust it off, and then make it available for public consumption. Many words have multiple meanings which do not always reflect the significance of the ideas they denote.

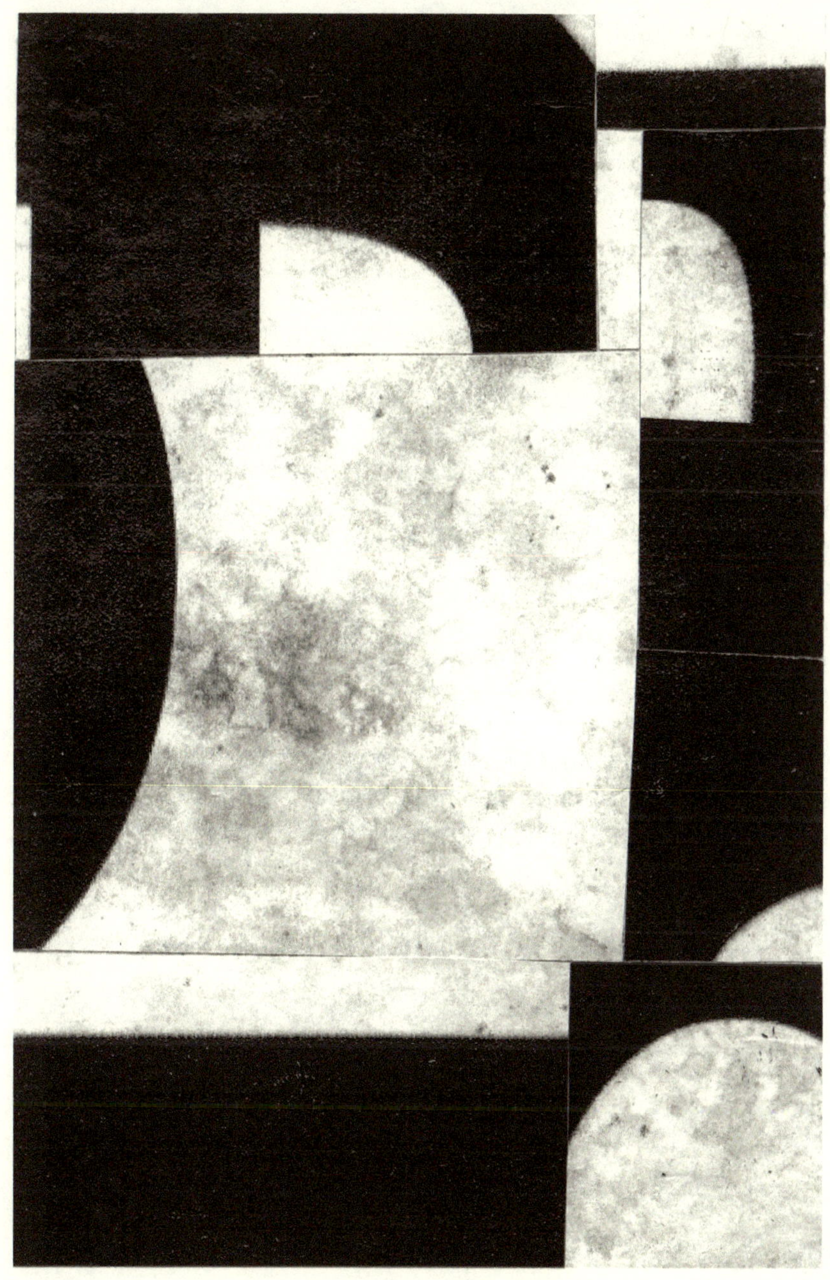

Plate 42

42

Monty Cantsin's Commentary:

Neoism: the problem is not the word but the nature of the concept denoted by the word. Neoism is paradoxical, illusive and complex, and yet, what a challenge! It is an inquiry into a dead end, but it does not have to end there. Vague, illusive and paradoxical as the concept may be – Neoism is nonetheless the essence of experience.

Karen Eliot's Commentary

Neoism is a conceptual blind spot in philosophical inquiry that reveals the intertwinements of conceptions of lived realities that are organized with the help of categories.

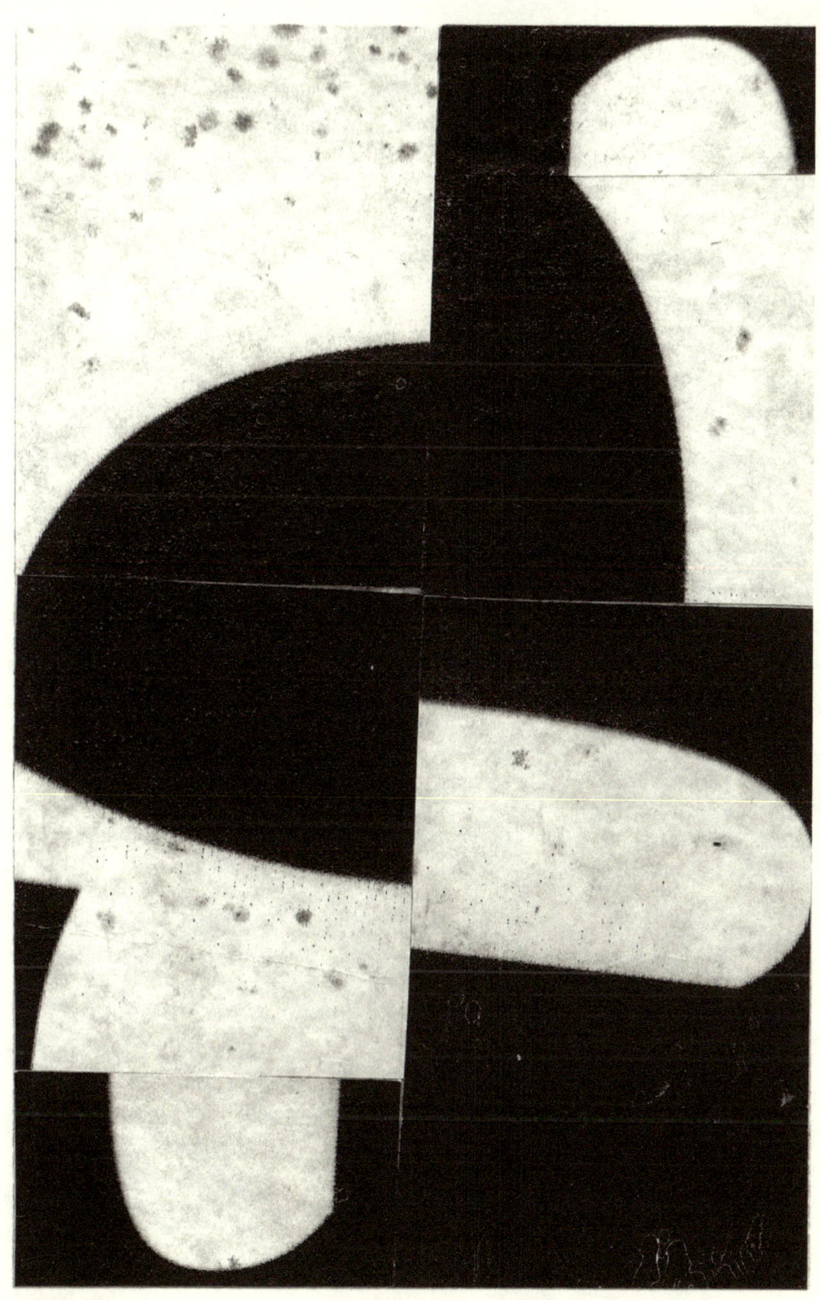

Plate 43

43

Monty Cantsin's Commentary:

Neoists evade the normativity that takes shape within a network of relationships. Whose lives are understood to qualify as our own after all?

Karen Eliot's Commentary

In the context of asymmetrical power relations Neoists give carte blanche to whiter teeth and fashionable clothing – especially designer blue jeans.

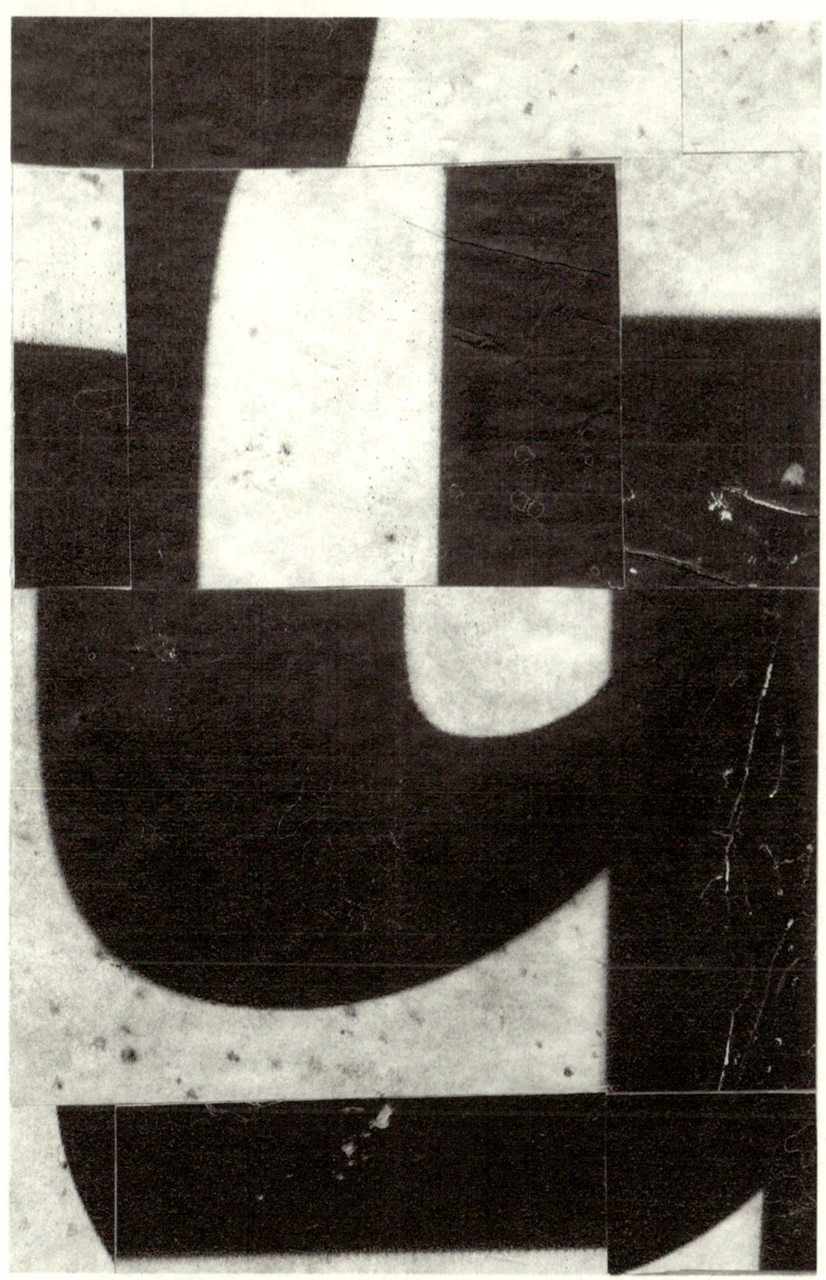

Plate 44

Monty Cantsin's Commentary:

Neoist structures of relationality enable and constrain possibilities for aesthetic intersubjectivity and exchange.

Karen Eliot's Commentary

A long time ago Plato observed that truth does not reside in the visible. The Neoist avoids getting dazed by the external aspects of things, in order to perceive the "cupness" of the cup, the "chairness" of the chair. All things specific are based on archetypes of a more general nature.

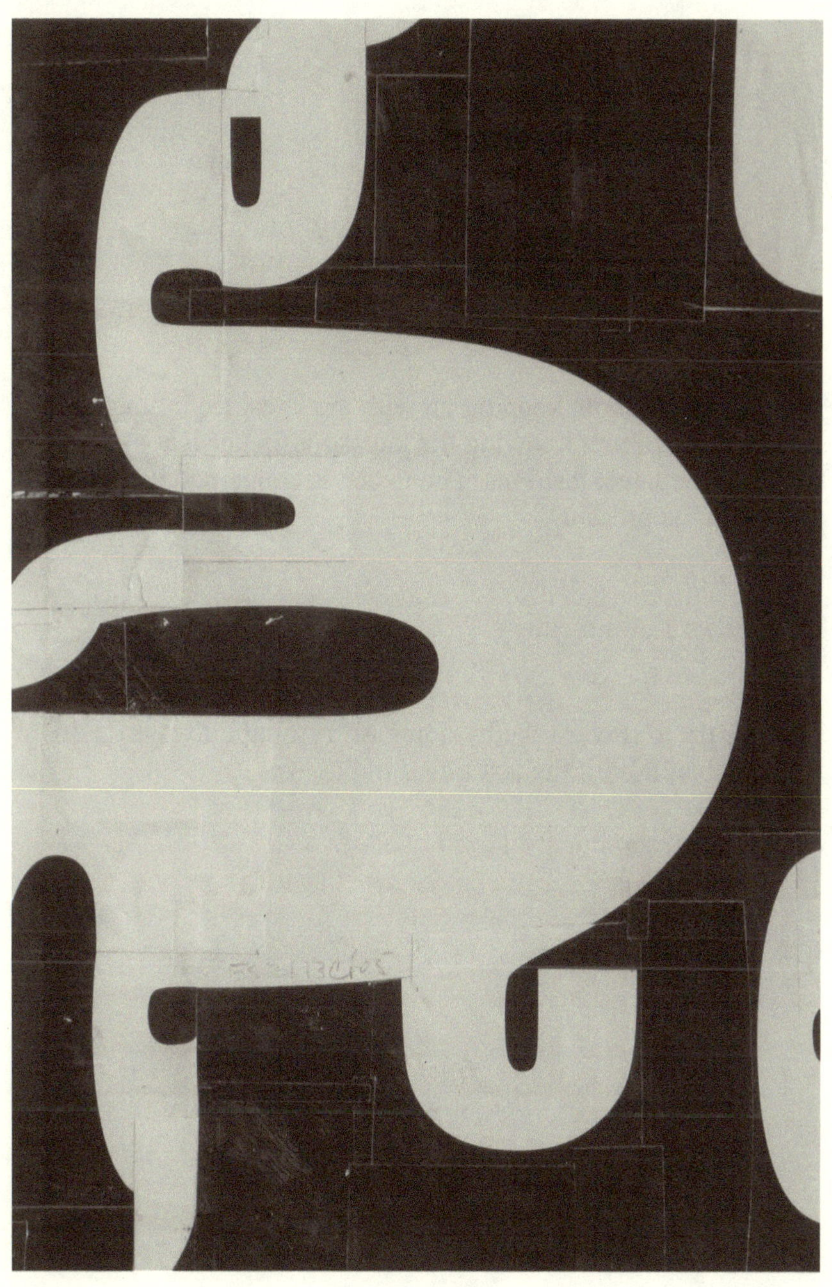

Plate 45

45

Monty Cantsin's Commentary:

Neoism is not about keeping up with the latest technological advances, not about knowing the latest gossip nor is it about adhering to the latest fashions. The neoist is concerned with being present in the present.

Karen Eliot's Commentary

I always try to stay awake by doing everything I always do differently than I did it the last time I did it.

Once awake, staying awake is not easy.

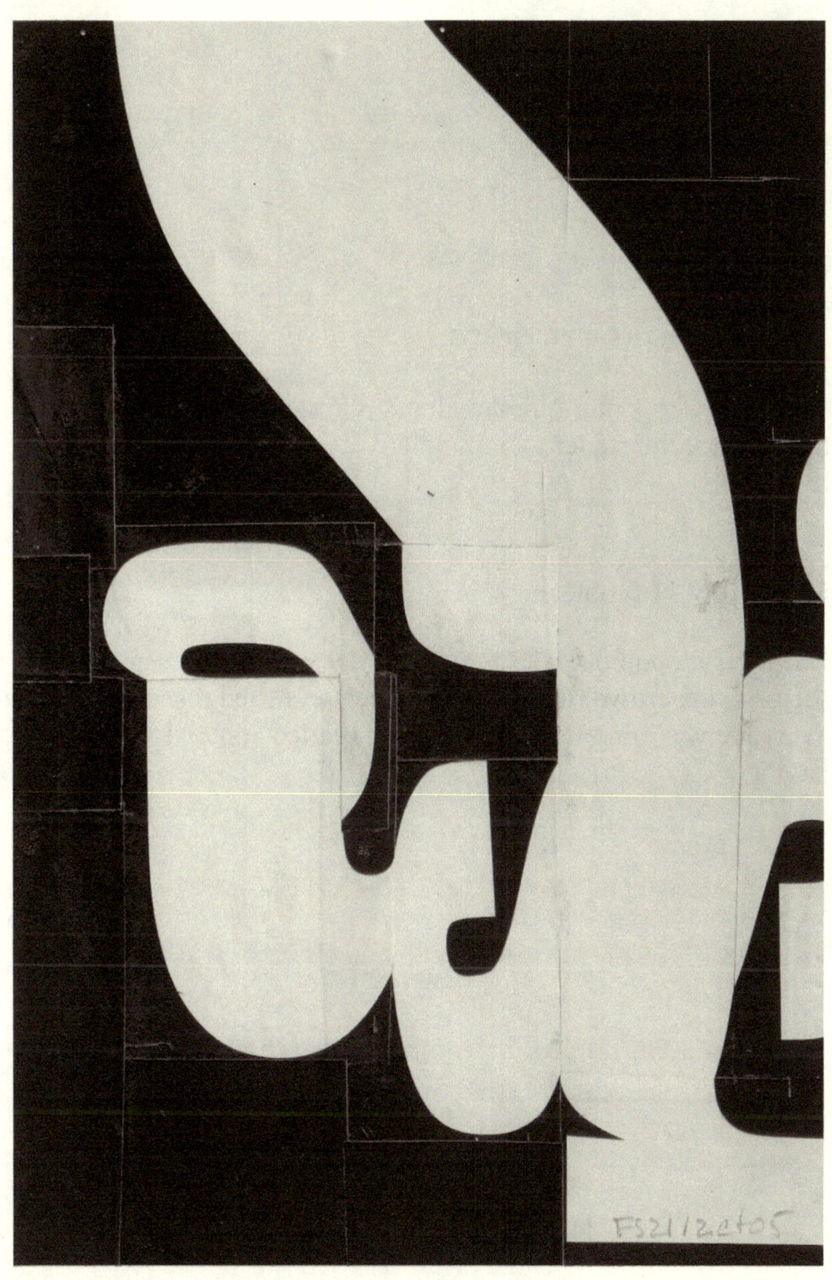

Plate 46

Monty Cantsin's Commentary:

The manifesto's non-referentialness & fragmentation are meant to stimulate the reader to extrapolate & explore the text creatively.

Karen Eliot's Commentary

Use a very loud boat horn to warn others of one's presence in the fog or in the crowd of a large discothèque. I tried this once and everyone was annoyed with what they called "obnoxious" behavior.

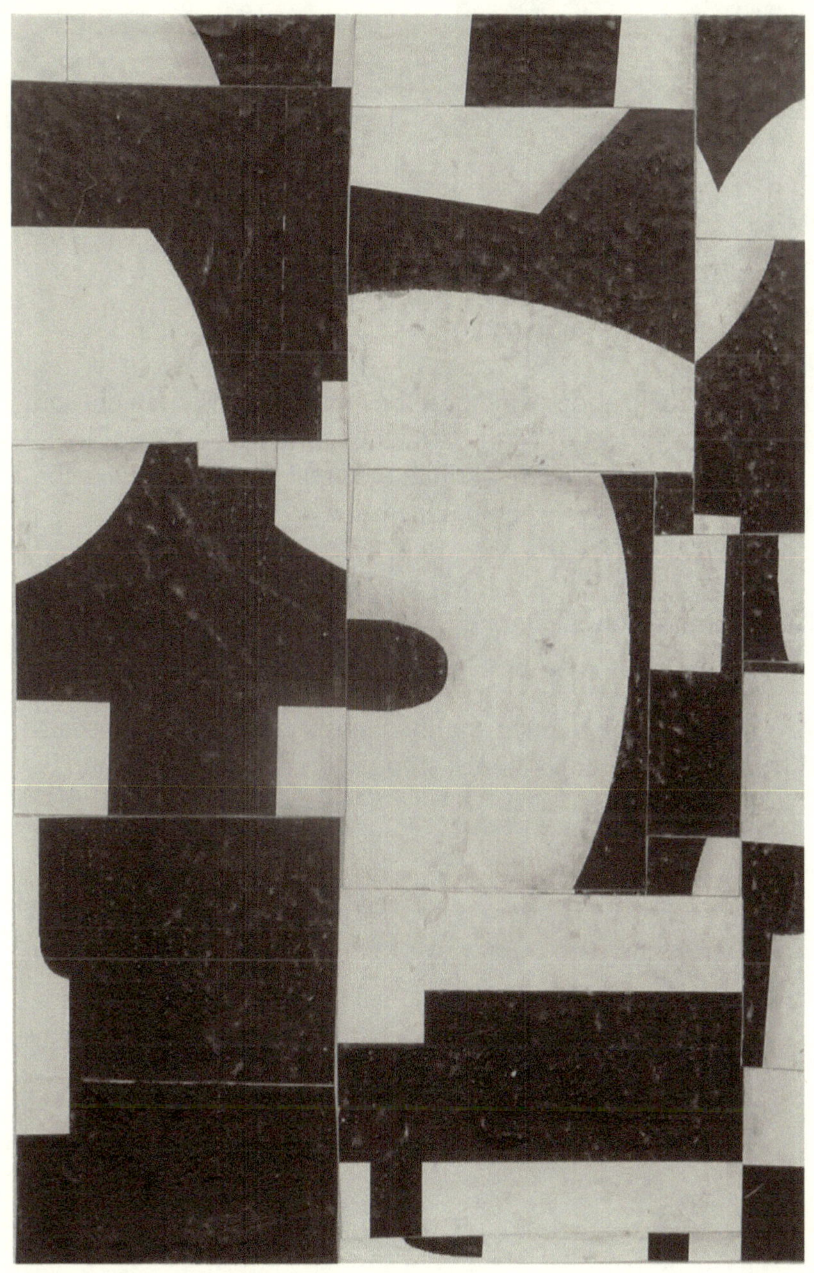

Plate 47

47

Monty Cantsin's Commentary:

There is a realization, which can be cultivated, wherein one can calculate the effect of Neoist strategy. All mechanisms of logic are broken, control is impossible, the great confusion rules: the search for meaning through vulnerability

Karen Eliot's Commentary

Any definition of Neoism simultaneously reveals and conceals. It has changed peoples' plans; stopped their progress dead in its tracks.

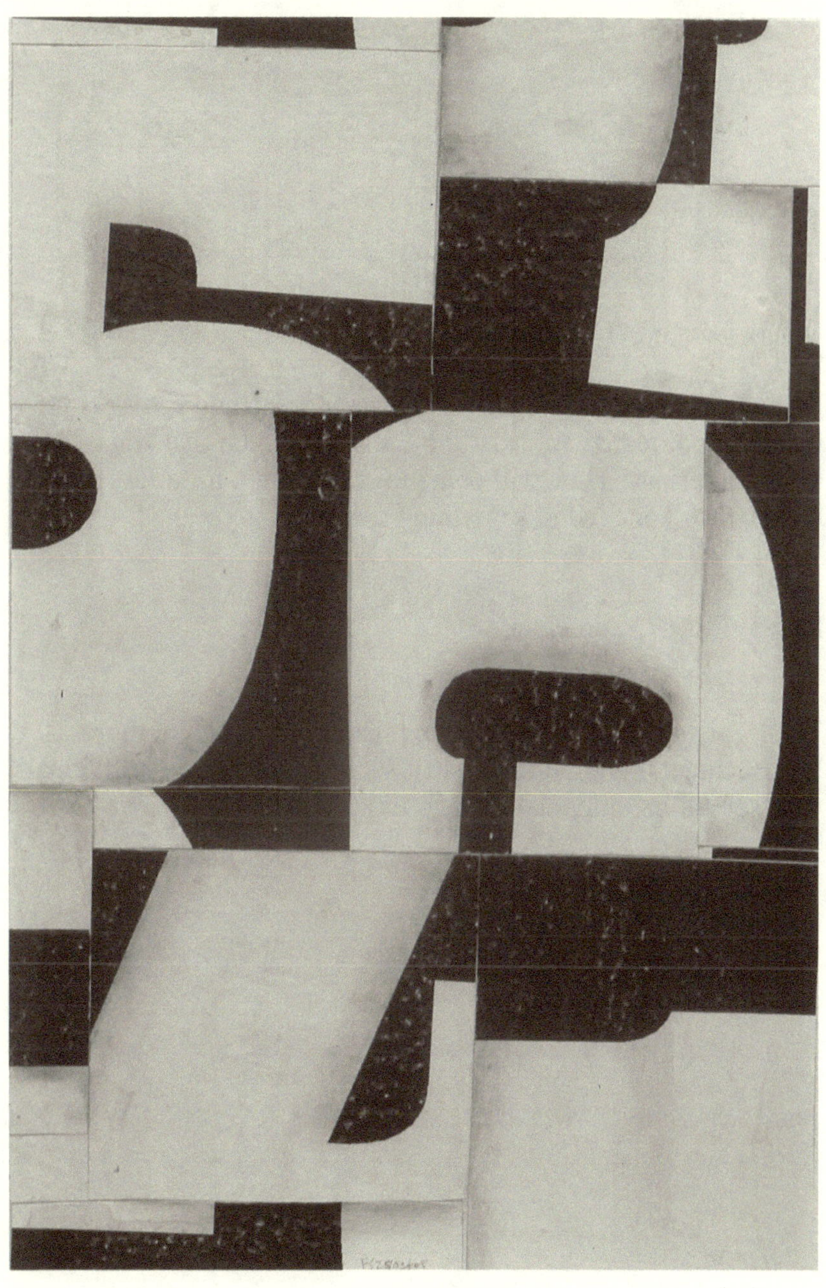

Plate 48

Monty Cantsin's Commentary:

Don't engage in Neoist activity for other artists, do it for people who will not realize (at least for a few moments) that what you have done is art. They will come to realize that, for a few moments, they believed in something extraordinary.

Karen Eliot's Commentary

The Neoists seems comically simplistic. When two or more Neoists meet it is time for a party. Neoists are simply individuals with something unnamable in common.

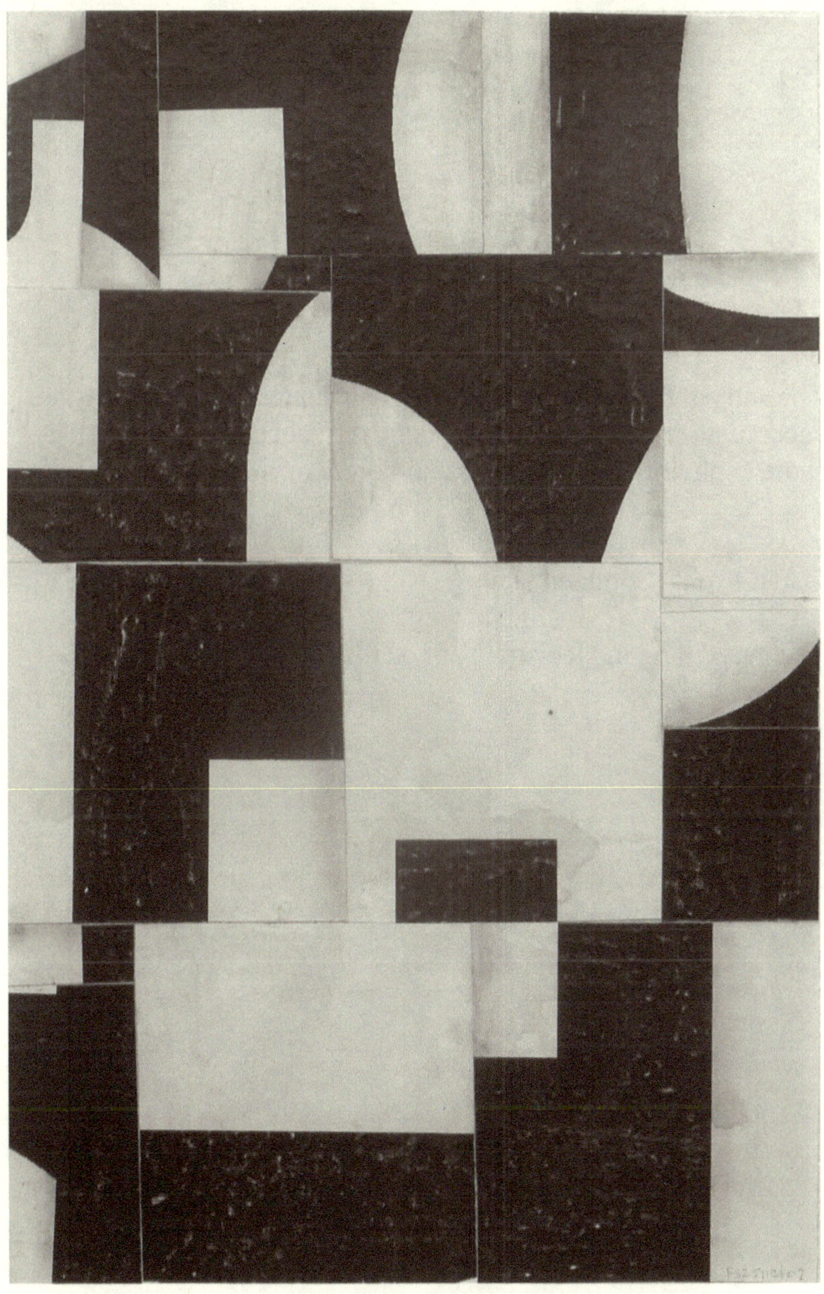

Plate 49

49

Monty Cantsin's Commentary:

The subject has no importance, logic is unnecessary, there is an accumulation of well-known things, the focus is always on the same explicit facts, repetition and boredom rule.

Karen Eliot's Commentary

Not everything in Neoism is of equal value.

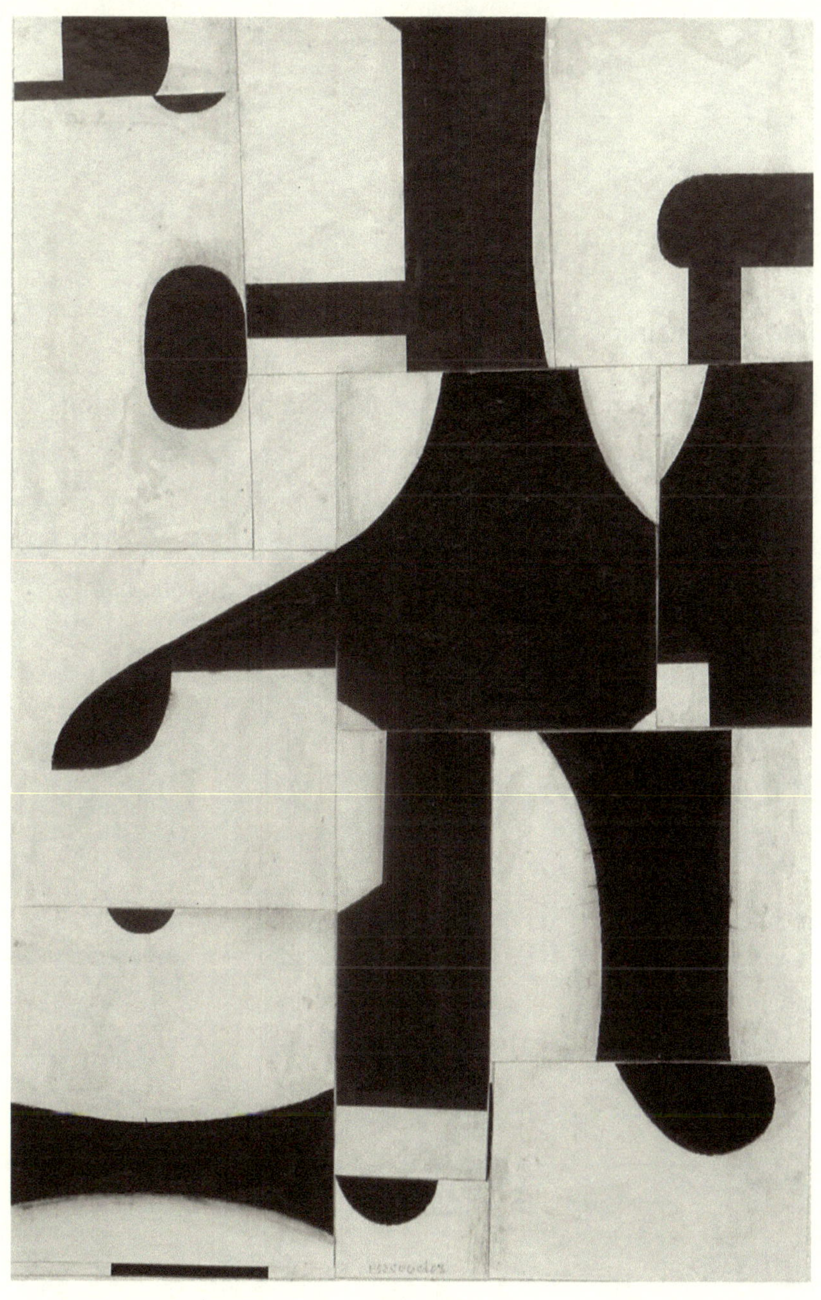

Plate 50

Monty Cantsin's Commentary:

Neoism: the mere act of giving it a name implies falsification.

Karen Eliot's Commentary

Information is a bank that we have to force open in the name of a free admittance.

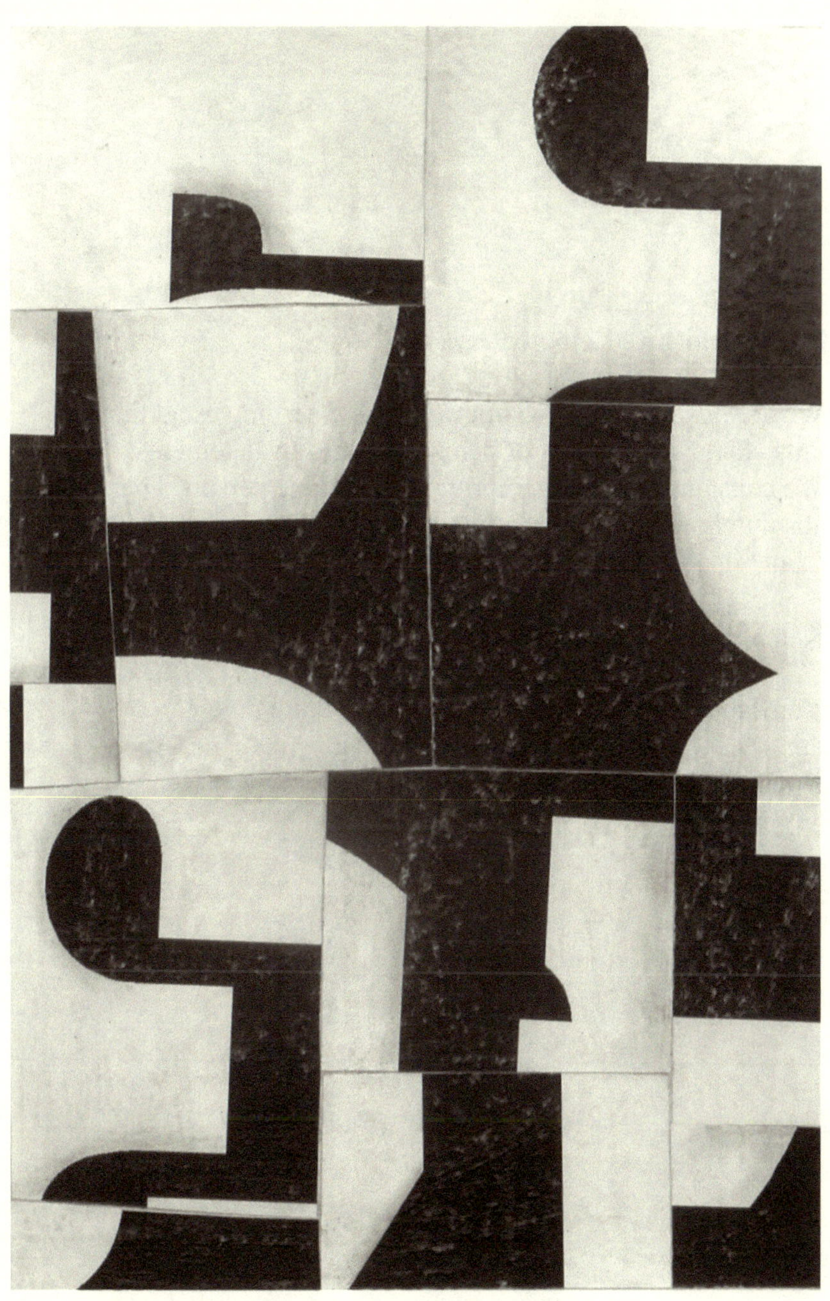

Plate 51

51

Monty Cantsin's Commentary:

We are pushing the envelope which is emerging as adding details, distortions--shifts of perspectives, rearrangements.
We constantly strive to improve the average person. There are absolutely no laws prohibiting participation and I really mean that.

Karen Eliot's Commentary

You can add something else, take something down,
I'm just following my thoughts where they take me.
No more rules, no headaches, what ever you want!

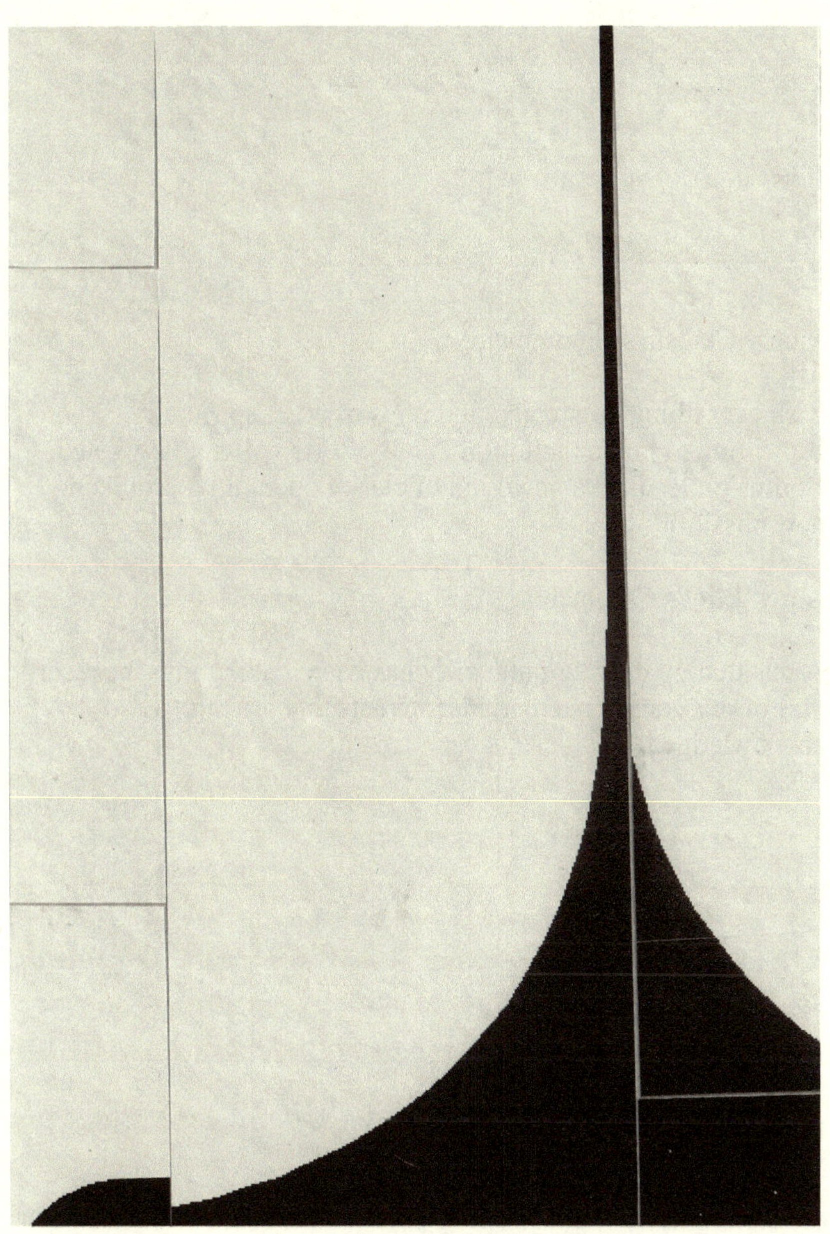

Plate 52

Monty Cantsin's Commentary:

Risk everything poetically, and most of all.... spiritually.
Be willing to pursue intuition. Your efforts will not be wasted.
Confusion leads to a new kind of clarity opening to promising new possibilities.

Karen Eliot's Commentary

A maddening quantum unreality has been leaking into the reservoir of our common experience: events that are rarely acknowledged.

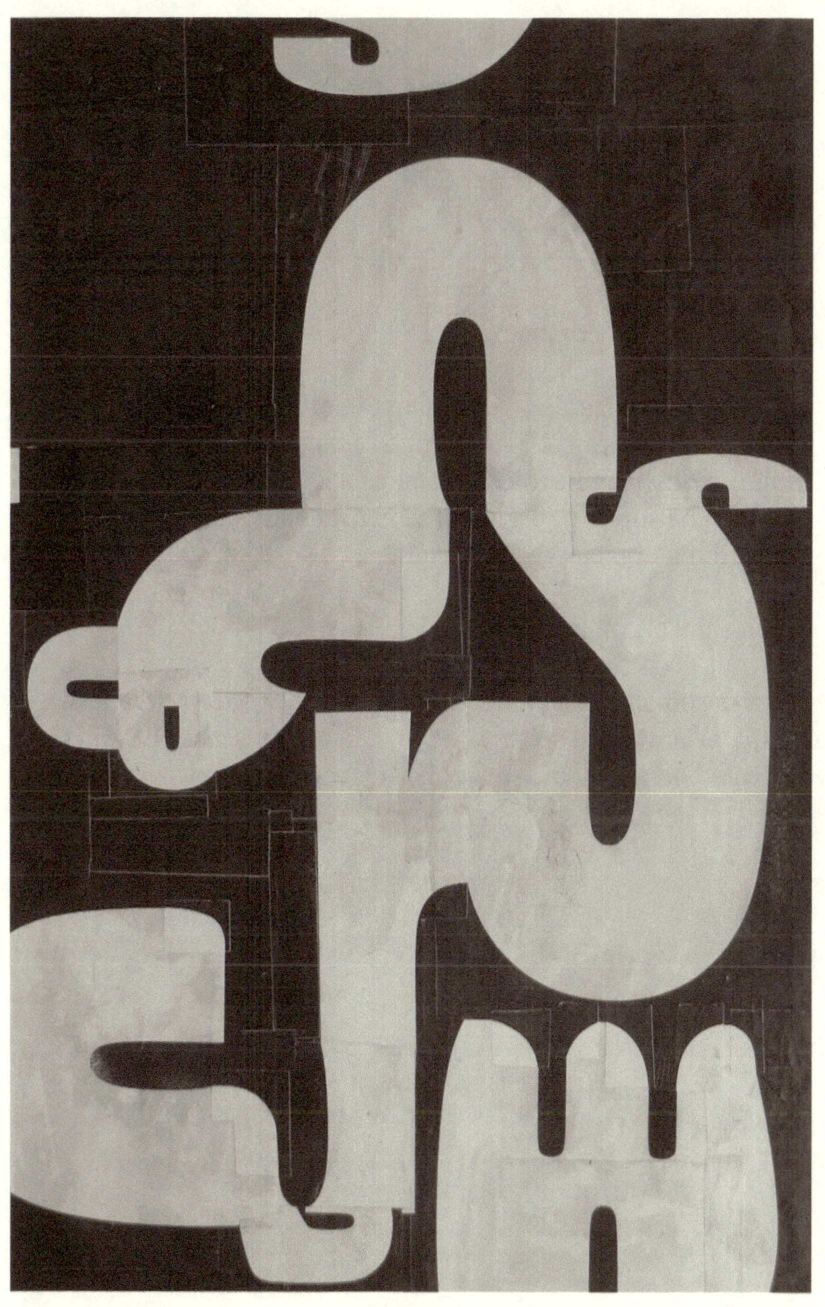

Plate 53

53

Monty Cantsin's Commentary:

The universe is - in fact - in a state of collapse. We are so accustomed to the pressure. Everything seems to be continually ending. “How can I avoid these pops and clicks?” You might ask. It is the sound of digital dreams. Whether you think you can or you think you can't, you're right.

Karen Eliot's Commentary

There is something about collecting and categorizing that gives a feeling of order and security on one hand, but seems sick and demented on the other.

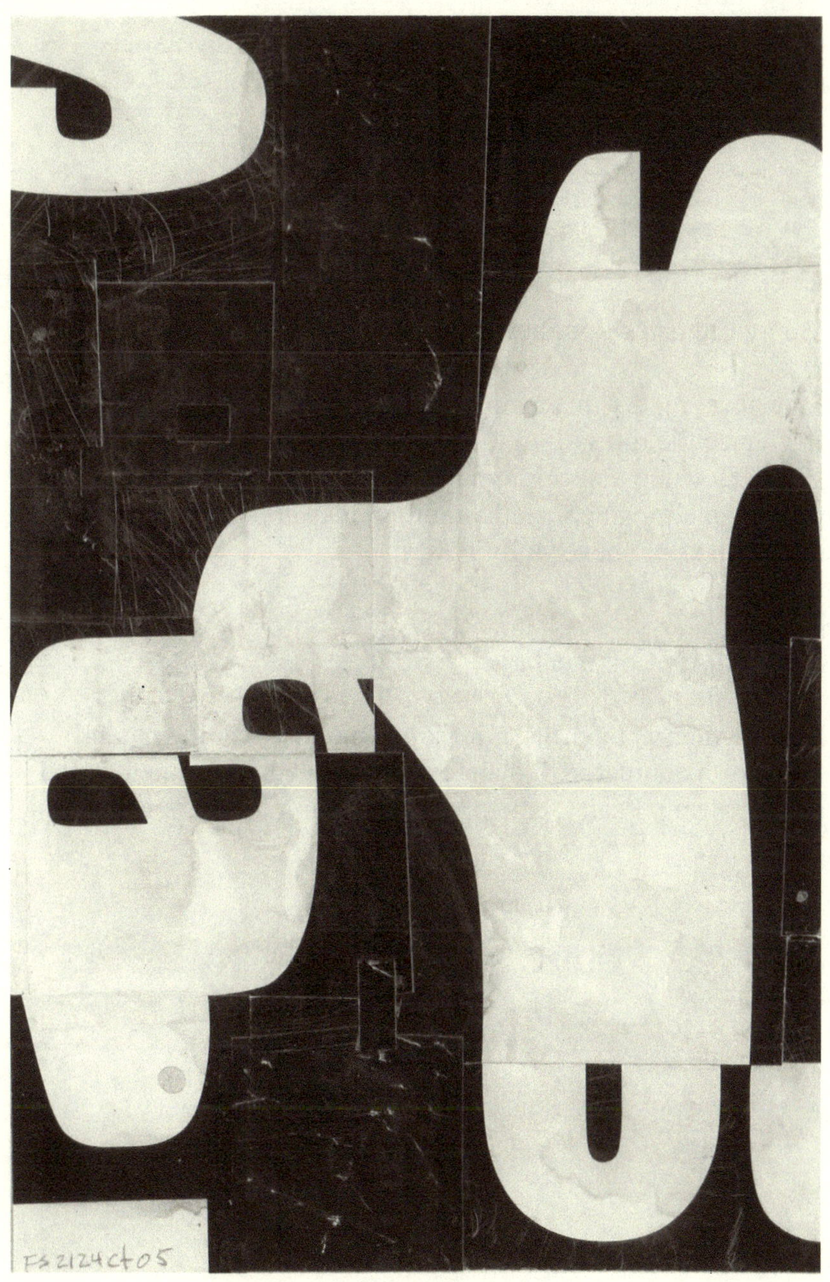

Plate 54

Monty Cantsin's Commentary:

Transform reality in a manner that is aesthetically pleasing. Renounce the rules of logic and the strictness of scientific arrogance. Develop a new idiom. Rely on imagination. Development toward an aim which poetic intuition may apprehend, but which the intellect can never fully grasp.

Karen Eliot's Commentary

Destroy men's pretences at reason and rediscover the natural found or manufactured, plain or complicated, fault-tolerant and self-repairing. I can't remember ever having lived anywhere else.

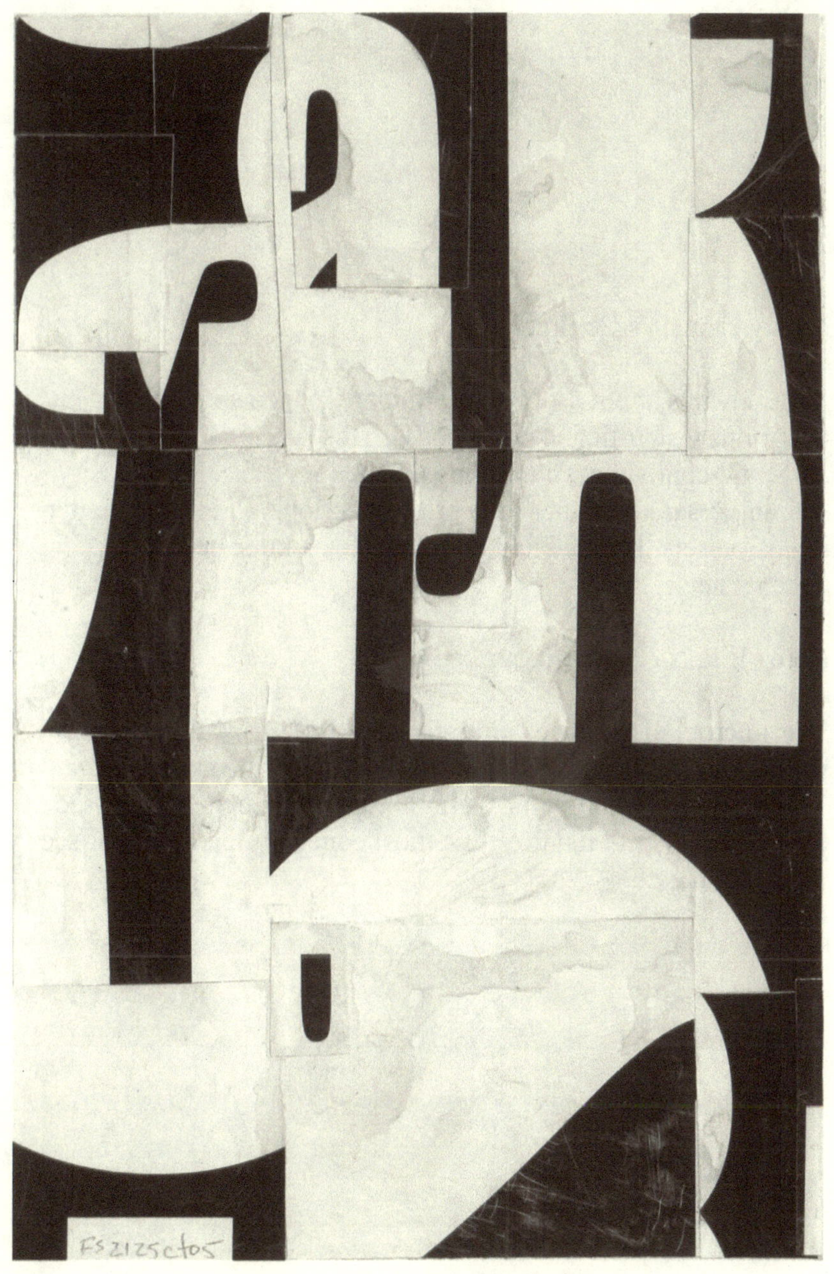

Plate 55

55

Monty Cantsin's Commentary:

Art is always about "something hidden". Place an emphasis on the primary significance of process. This is one of the more fundamental challenges in thinking and acting; a fact of necessity and universal law rather than prior intention, akin to the shattering of vessels. Isolated and closed systems must necessarily degenerate.

Karen Eliot's Commentary

Many actors of practices, initiatives and confrontations would just like to see art treated seriously. I think it's a stretch.
You have to feel that your "self" is capable of being expressed through paint, and manifest the most concentrated horror of seeing women eat!

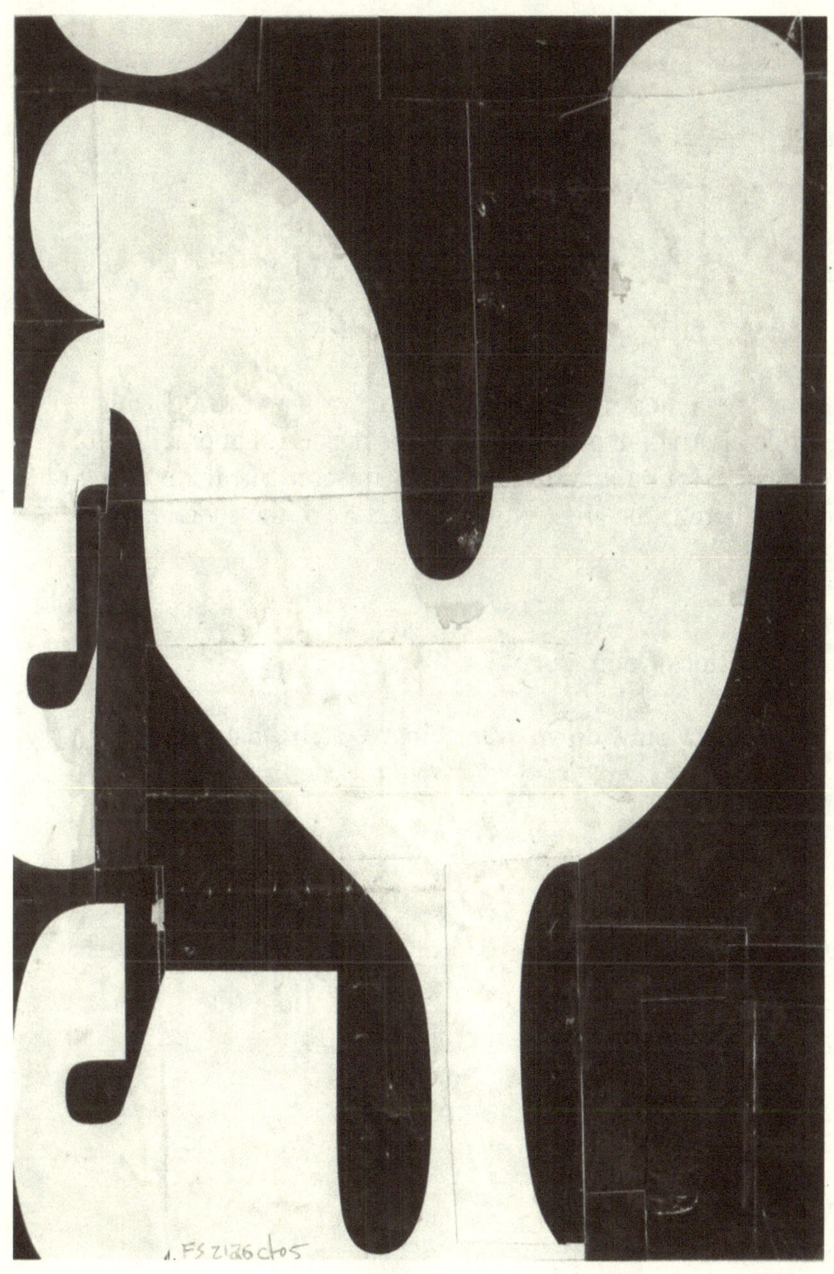

Plate 56

Monty Cantsin's Commentary:

Be at the center of the modern world, groom yourself with a strong alternative presence. Become masterful at practices of counter-information. Contentiously misconstrue the purpose of life. Where is the creativity of the actors of the social movements?

Karen Eliot's Commentary

Slow down. Slow down everything. Watch what happens.

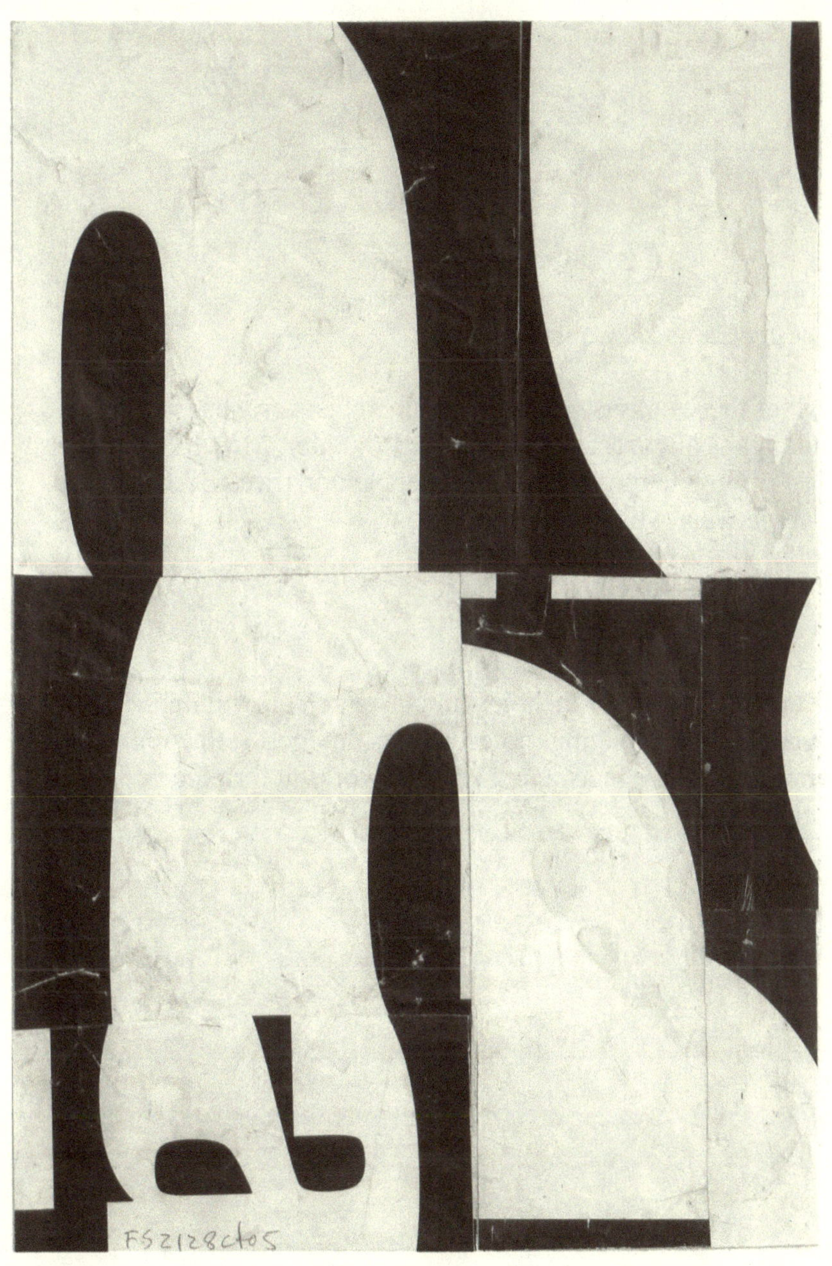

Plate 57

57

Monty Cantsin's Commentary:

All of these activists, protesters, anarchists or whatever..., hooligans all wearing Lee, Levis, Wrangler, Moschinos, Pepe's or Kalvin Kleins & remember: people don't wear like they are, people wear what they want to be.

Karen Eliot's Commentary

You will search for meaningful clusters. You will delineate. It could be fascinating: notes, stories, images, reflection, editorial, comments, facts, etc. I am still working thru the implications.

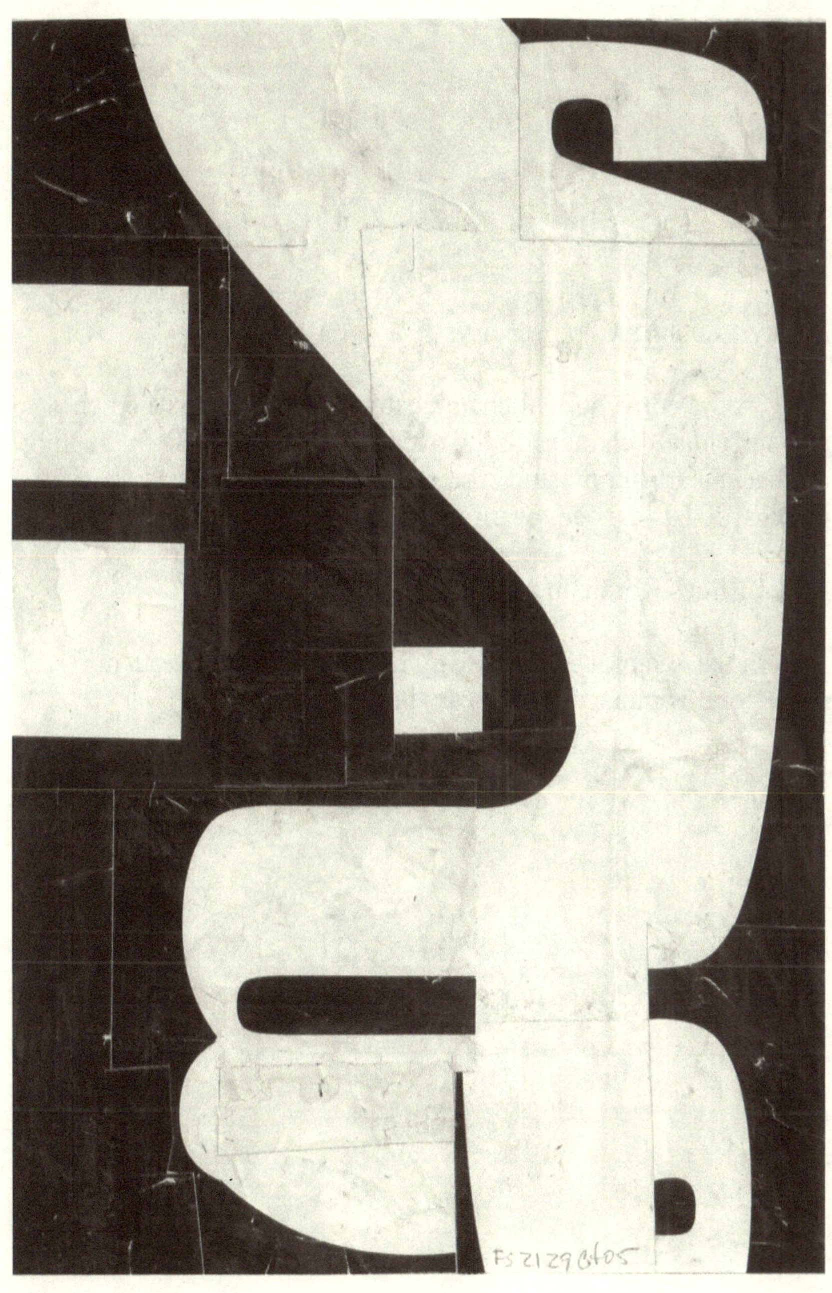

Plate 58

Monty Cantsin's Commentary:

Subvert the conventional channels by means of detournements and surrealistic changes of the events in order to raise the feeling of chaos, start rumors and spread waste which in their turn shall be regarded as carriers of information".

Karen Eliot's Commentary

Materialism cannot explain away its paradoxes. Advertising makes one popular. ‘Now’ is anybody's guess.

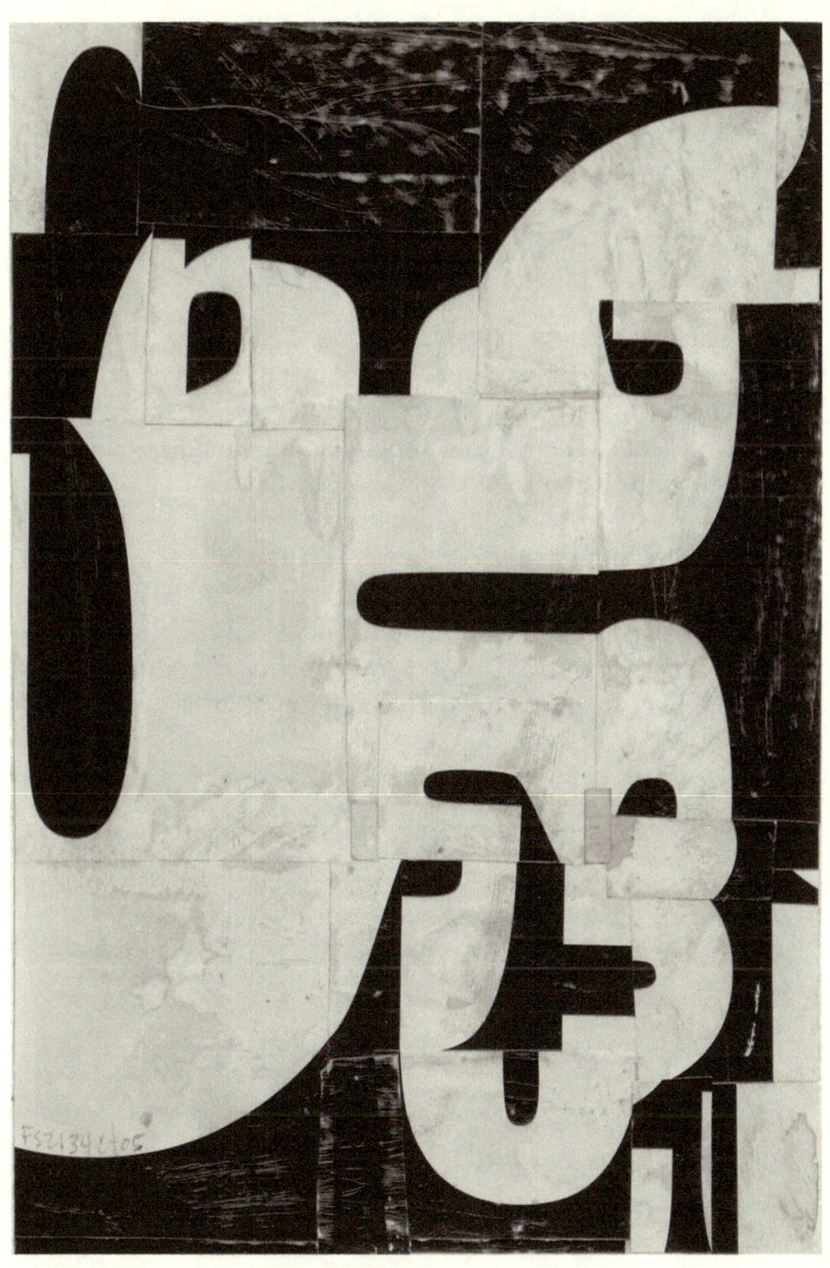

Plate 59

59

Monty Cantsin's Commentary:

I am reminded of secrets never intended to reach your eyes
the ever-present challenge to communicate. I would say this:
Pay attention, be astonished.

Karen Eliot's Commentary

I want to listen to good music, smell good smells, feel good textures, eat enjoyable foods, to find good quality reproductions, to buy and play with new toys. The creation of art is a very sensual experience.

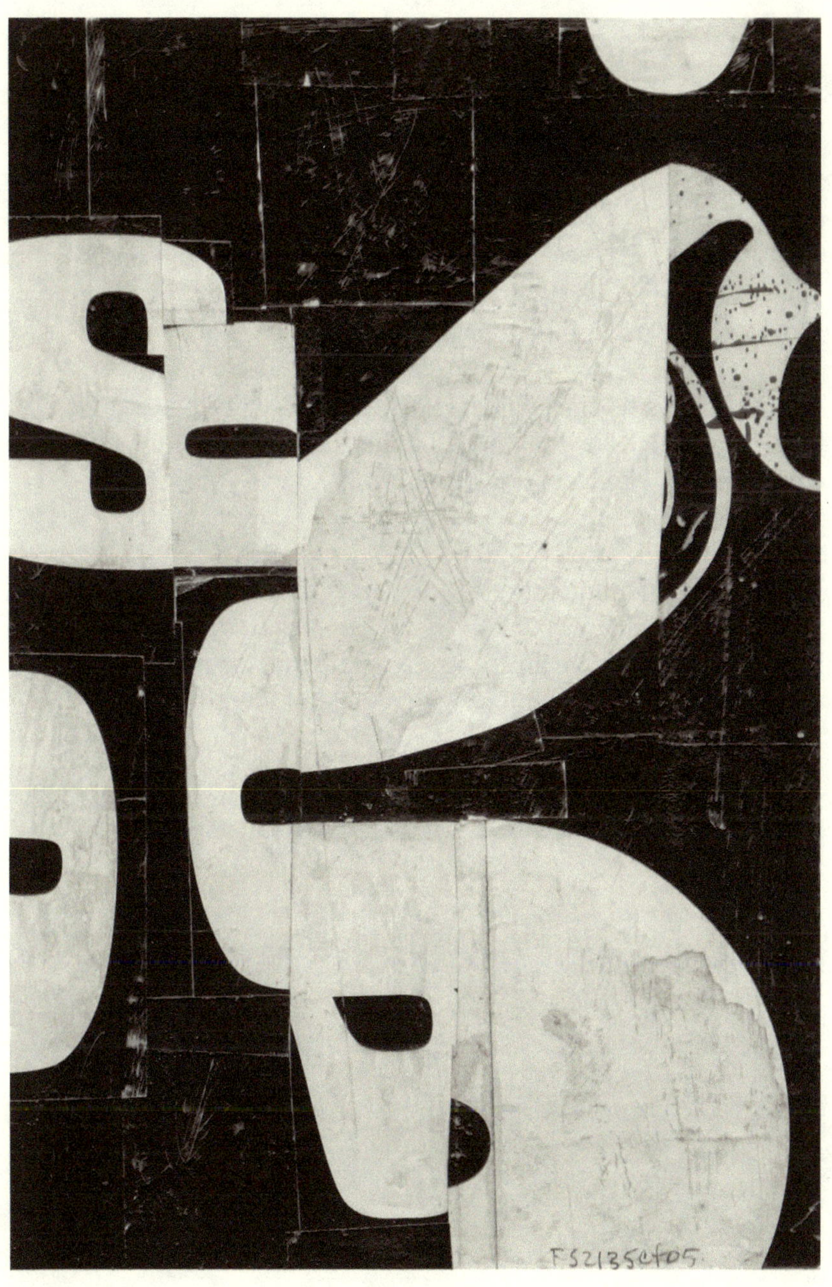

Plate 60

Monty Cantsin's Commentary:

Television has us chasing cars and clothes - working jobs we hate, to buy shit we don't need I am a sun god of golden rays and emptiness. Look closely, taste carefully, savor your life.

Karen Eliot's Commentary

I actually do not have an "e" in my name, the error occurred while processing an element with a general identifier.

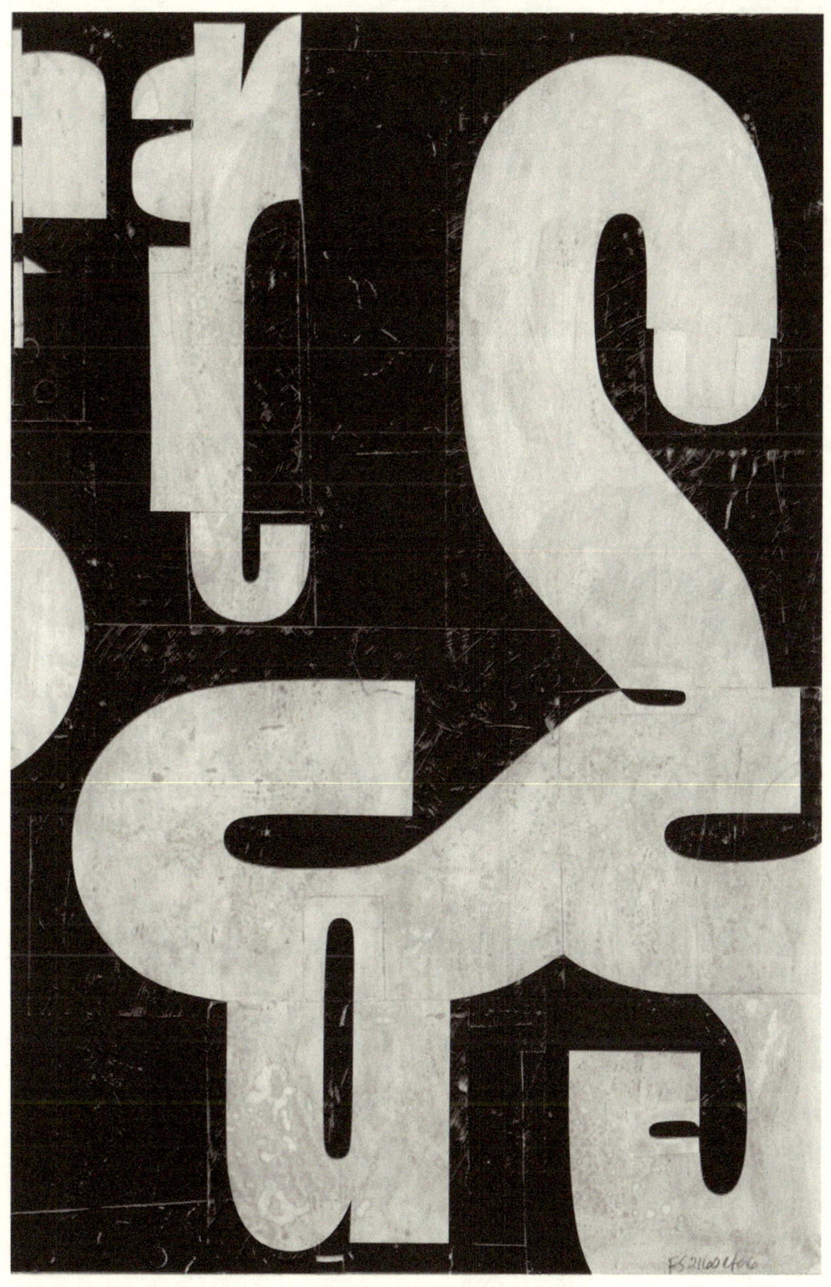

Plate 61

61

Monty Cantsin's Commentary:

There is no security, there is only opportunity.

Karen Eliot's Commentary

A television can function as a source of colorful ambient light... And everyone seems to like it! You have to put your mind 'somewhere else' so as not to panic or lose your breath.

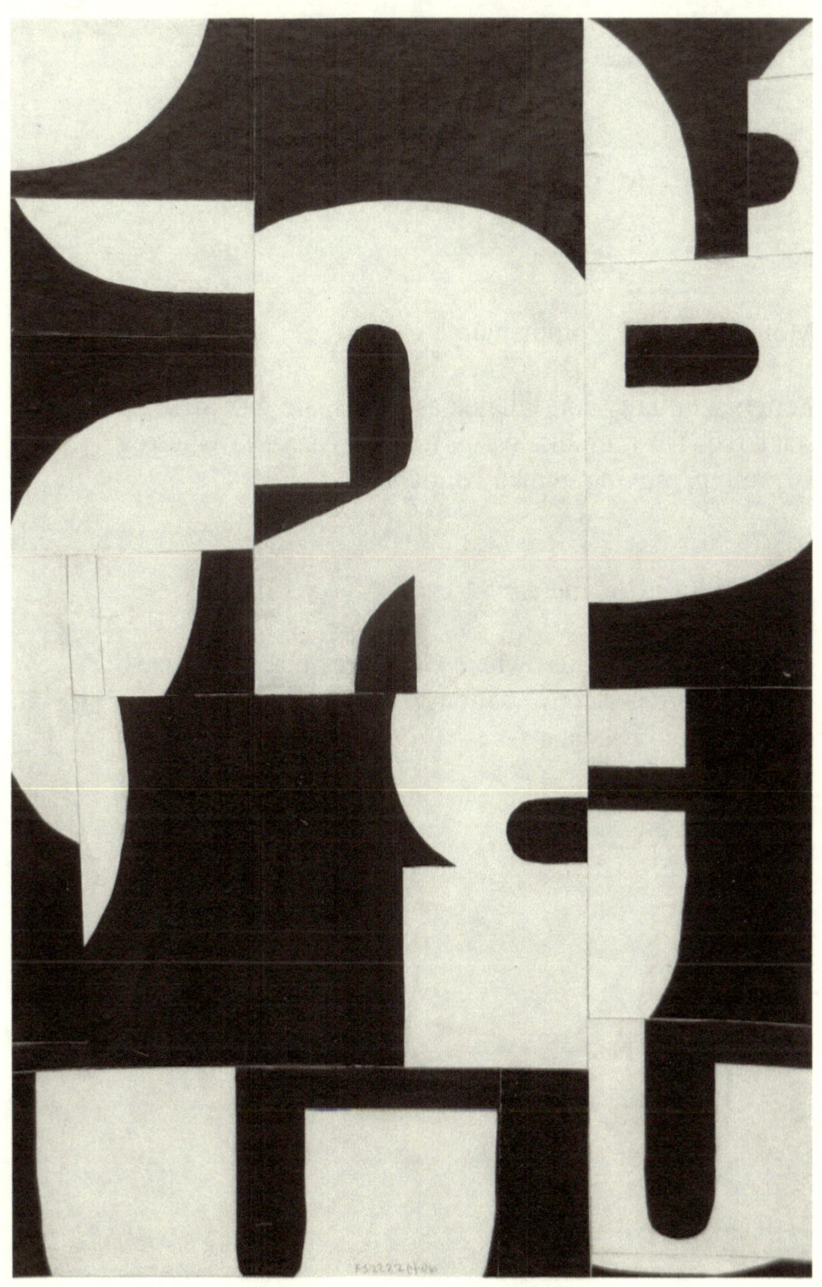

Plate 62

Monty Cantsin's Commentary:

Letters, normally constellated as words, are torn apart, scattered. They are like wasps and bees & yellow-jackets swarming, moving in many directions at once.

Karen Eliot's Commentary

Reading is always loss where we never quite recognize ourselves. There is a conversation of sorts in this; a sort of disposable conversation.

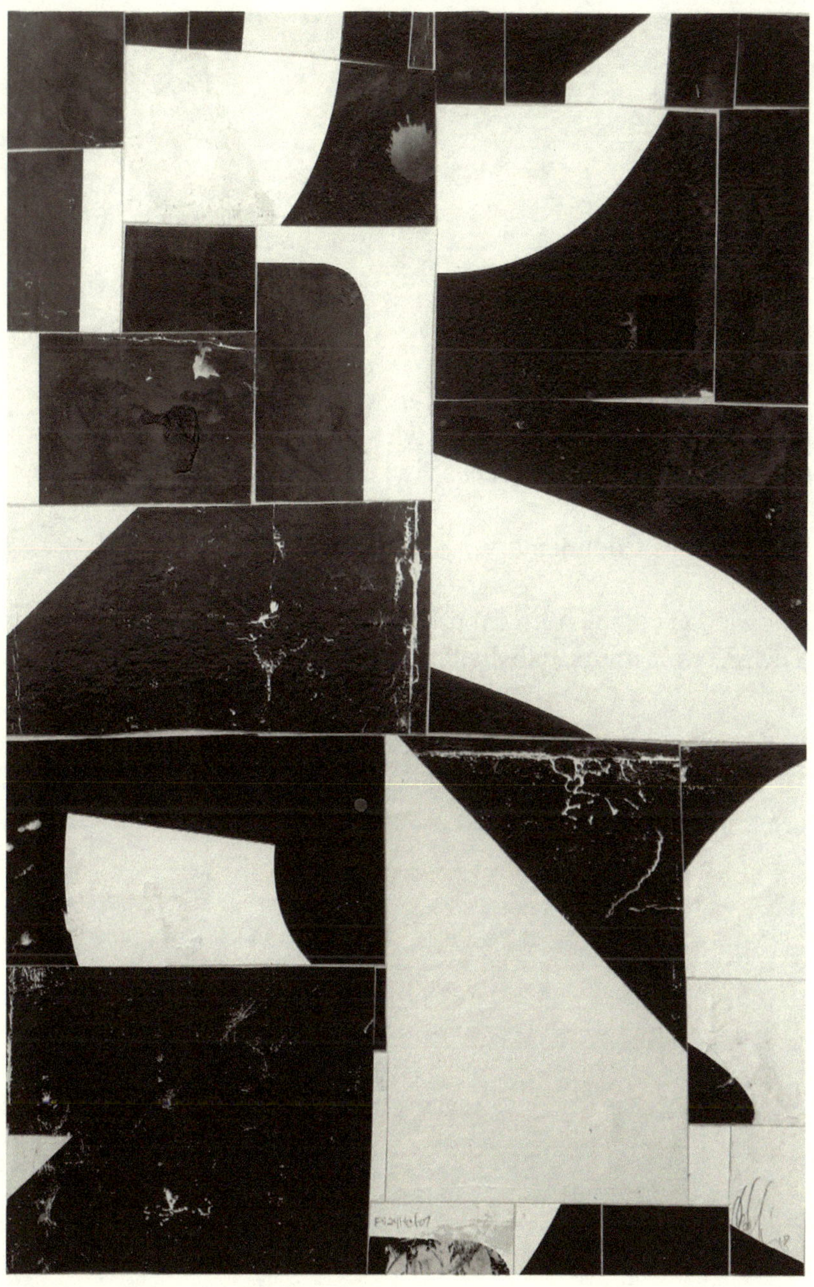

Plate 63

63

Monty Cantsin's Commentary:

Nobody can say they haven't been warned. Perhaps it's not surprising puzzling over past hairstyles. It's quite incredible just how destructive indecisiveness is.

Karen Eliot's Commentary

Knowledge comes from experience, skill from commitment. You are your limits. Challenge yourself daily.

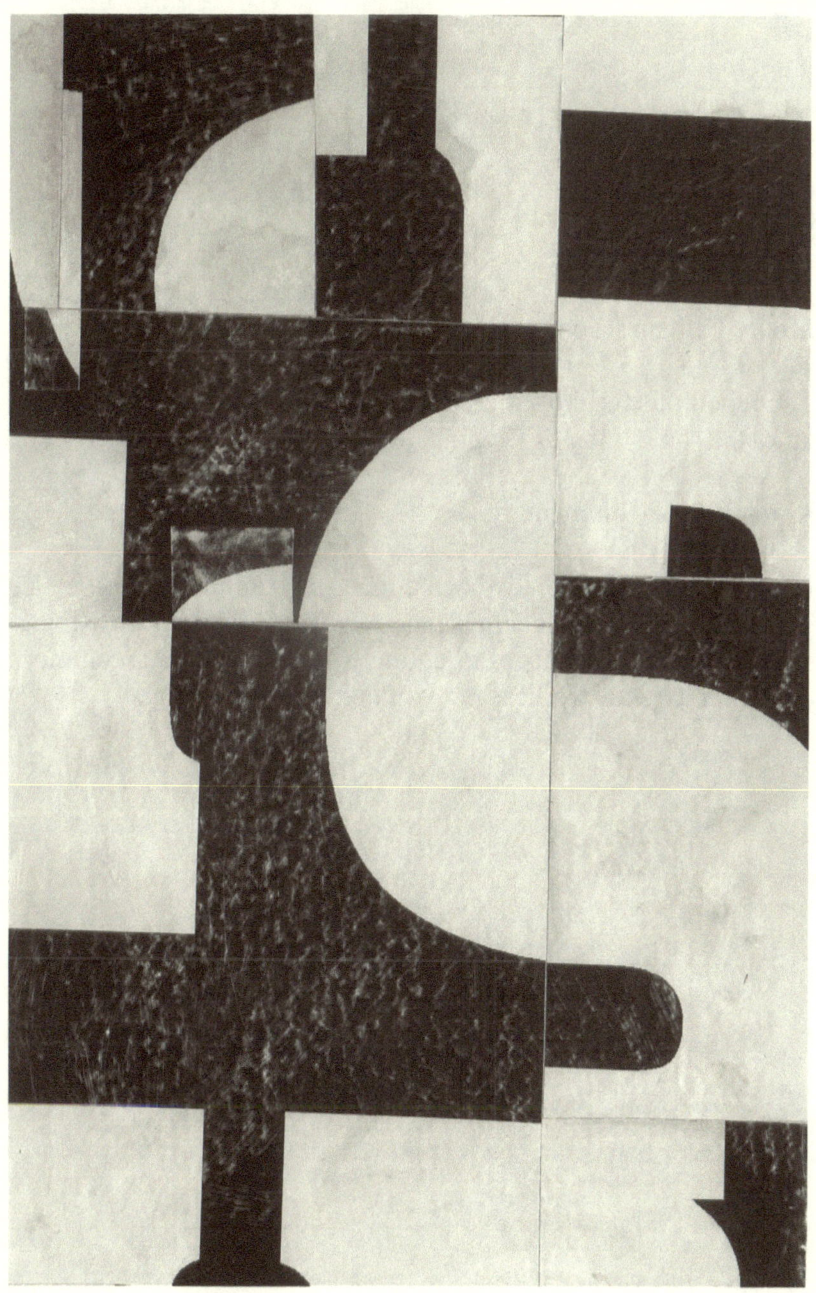

Plate 64

Monty Cantsin's Commentary:

The rebellious thrill of afternoon porn and Twinkies which isn't quite the same thing as keeping quiet.

Karen Eliot's Commentary

Maybe all this has already been done. Maybe not.
To assemble the whole – that's the part that is messy, obnoxious, smelly. Those moments of mingling with strangers, our common desire for a better world is nigh on to meaning nothing.

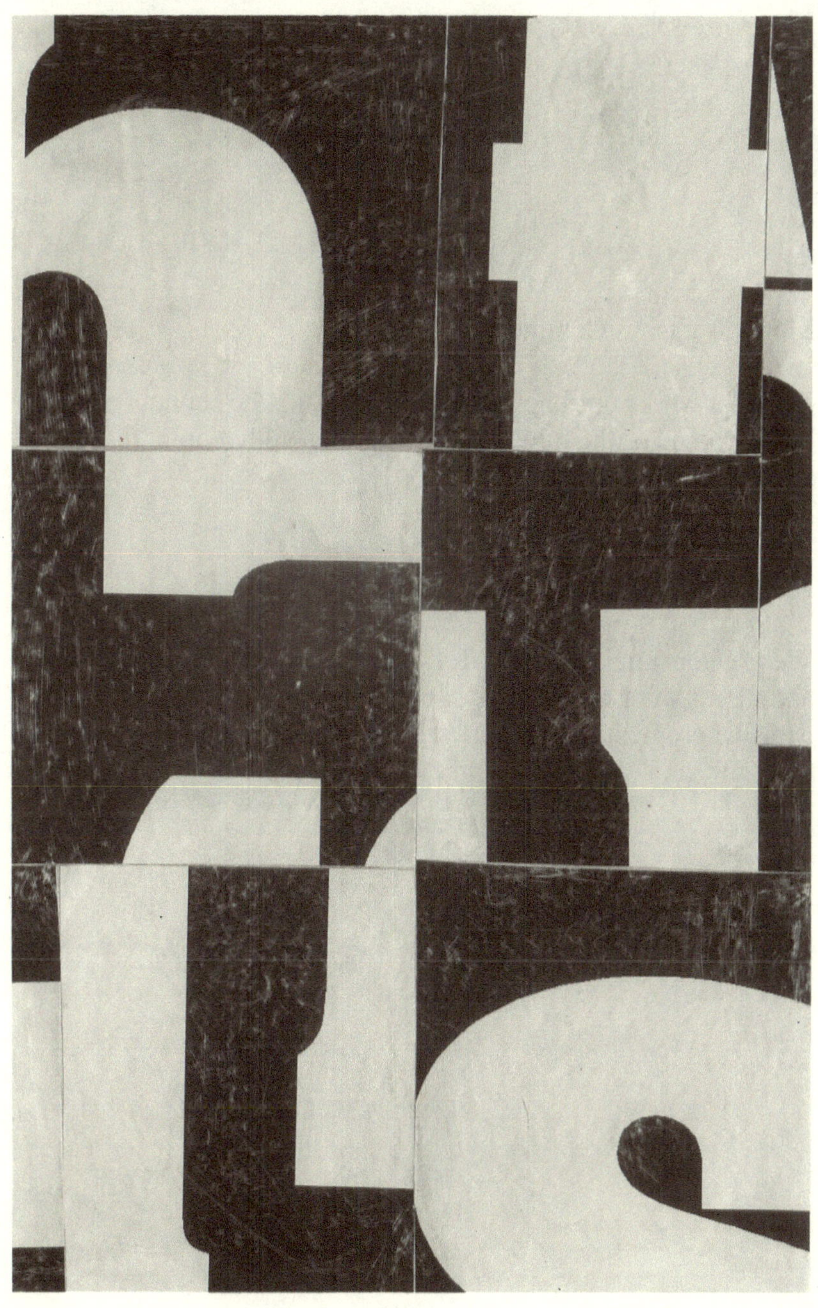

Plate 65

65

Monty Cantsin's Commentary:

An artist works until he gets to the point that he cannot remember the name of the thing he is doing. It is at that point that he is starting to make art.

Karen Eliot's Commentary

We use/consume/deliver "ART" day after day, week after week and month after month. It is simply untrue that we are making decisive progress. Art is a mystery and that's OK too.

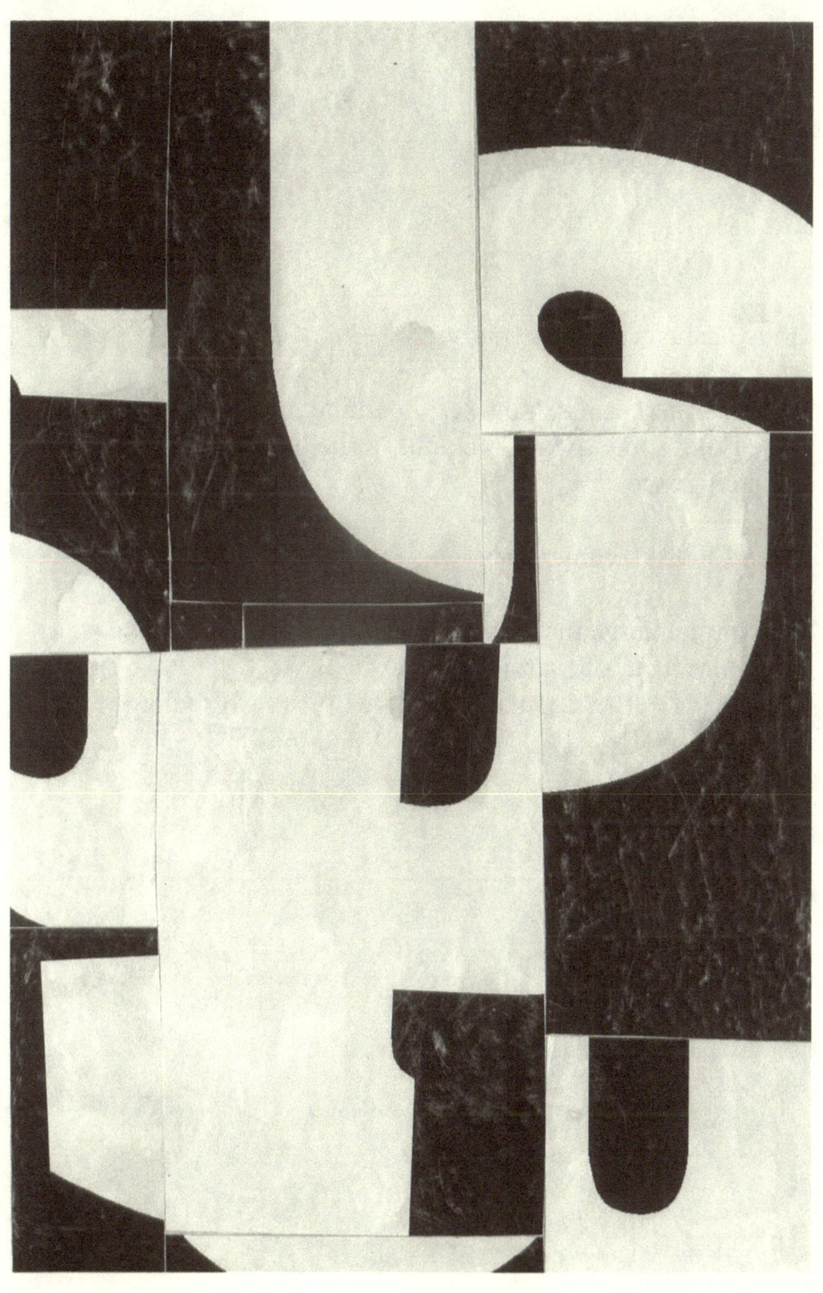

Plate 66

Monty Cantsin's Commentary:

Naturally there can be no rules. Learning to speak in a human voice is not some trick. Crank out sterile happytalk that insults the intelligence.

Karen Eliot's Commentary

The world at large may venerate and aspire to superlative super-luxury products and services.
Consequently, the essential objective of is to overindulge.

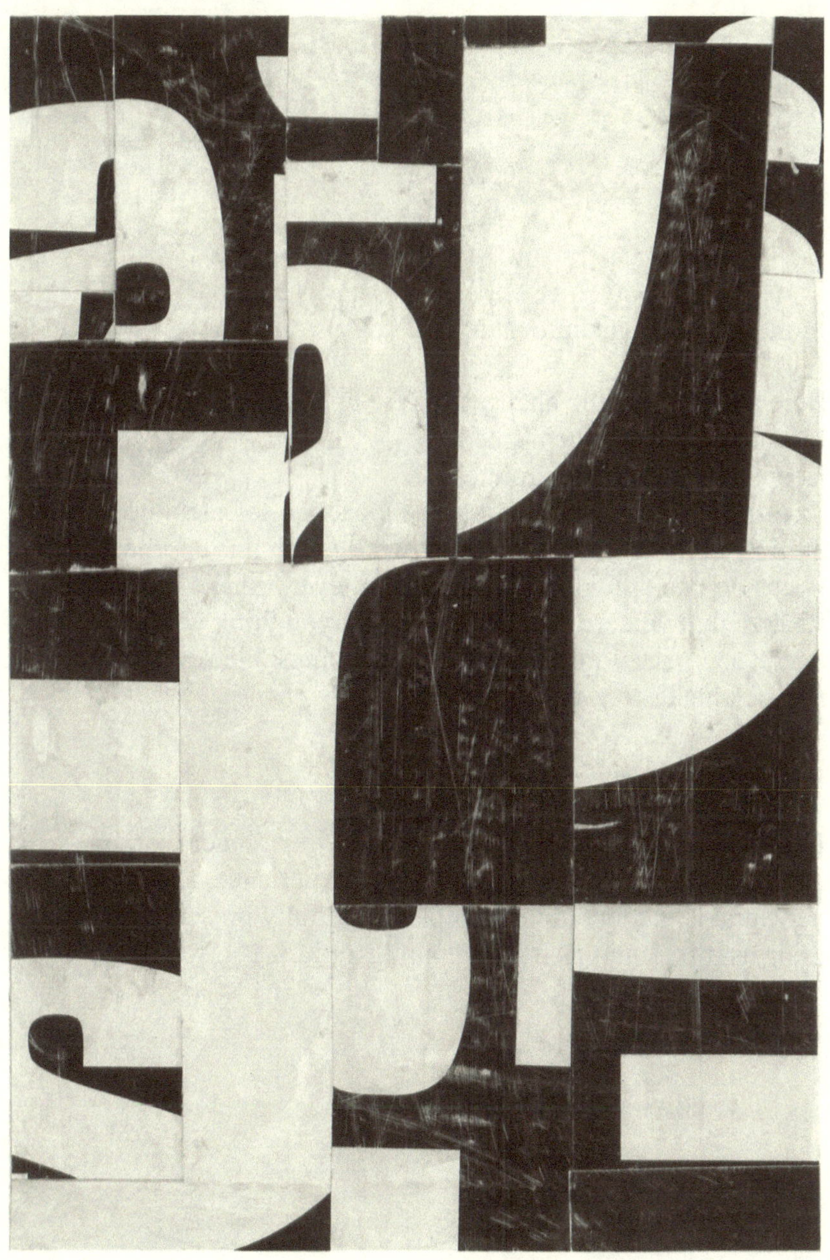

Plate 67

67

Monty Cantsin's Commentary:

Here are the key rule changes for the upcoming future.
If running, one can be tripped.
Keep both feet on the ground.
Excessive celebration going to the local pub to celebrate or celebrating too long, there is nothing wrong with this approach.
Focus on one thing to the exclusion of everything else.
Realize that you are not the person that you think you are.
Secret societies, lobbying efforts, snubbings, blackballings,
no one outside knew the rule.

Karen Eliot's Commentary

I have been practicing to learn about my own inner workings. There is nothing esoteric about it. My experience, and it may not be yours, is that practicing simply being fully present to everything as it is, is not a strong enough word for it.

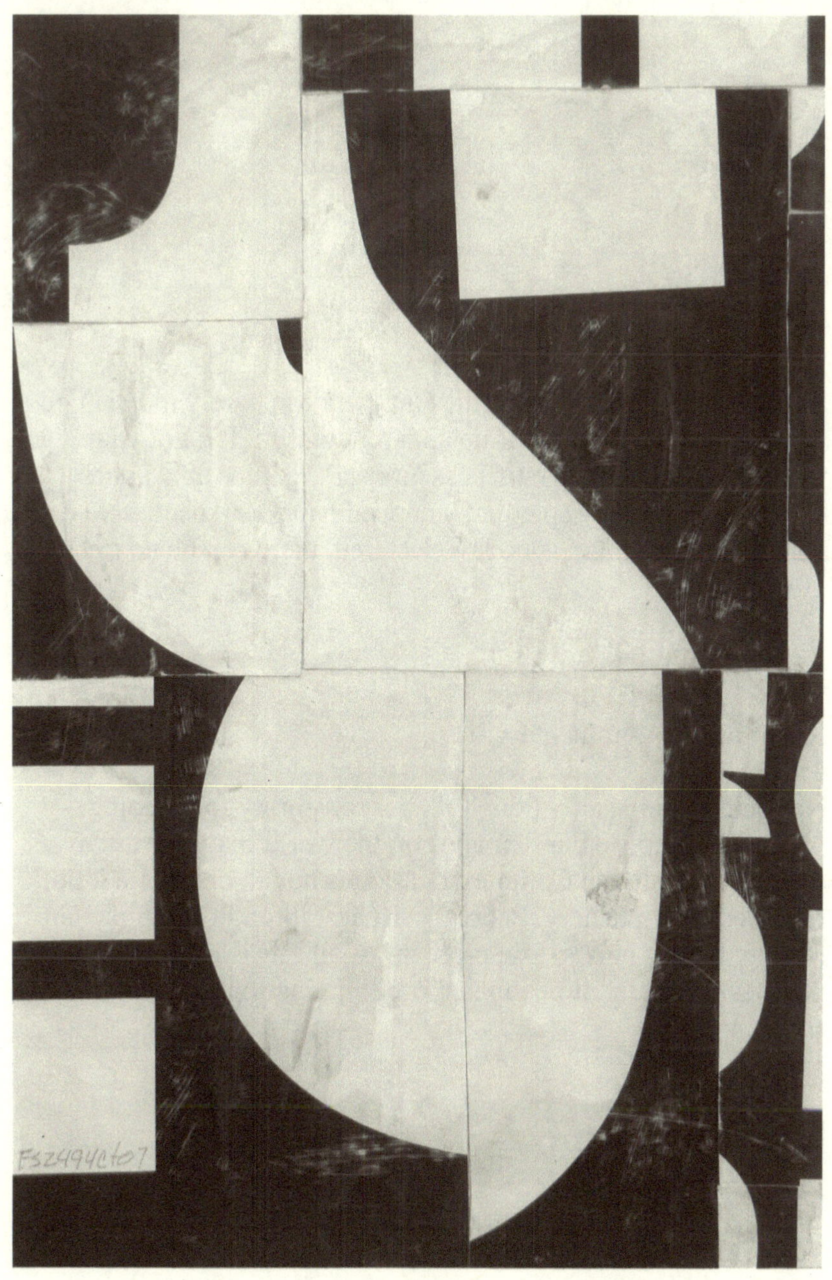

Plate 68

Monty Cantsin's Commentary:

You're so hemmed in with rules that you can barely move. You may have created rules for no apparent reason. It's not your fault. If you have pain, stiffness or swelling, pips and stones should be discreetly spat into a cupped hand in a dismissive fashion. Where there is no law declared, there can be no transgression.

Karen Eliot's Commentary

Noticing requires attention. Take responsibility for keeping watch. We impose our demands on the world that it be as we would wish it to be. Complexification is not an option - a lot of rehashed faux-poshery. People learn best through listening, not reading boring books. The problem is, all this is inherently obnoxious. Wouldn't it be much more illuminating to learn something new?

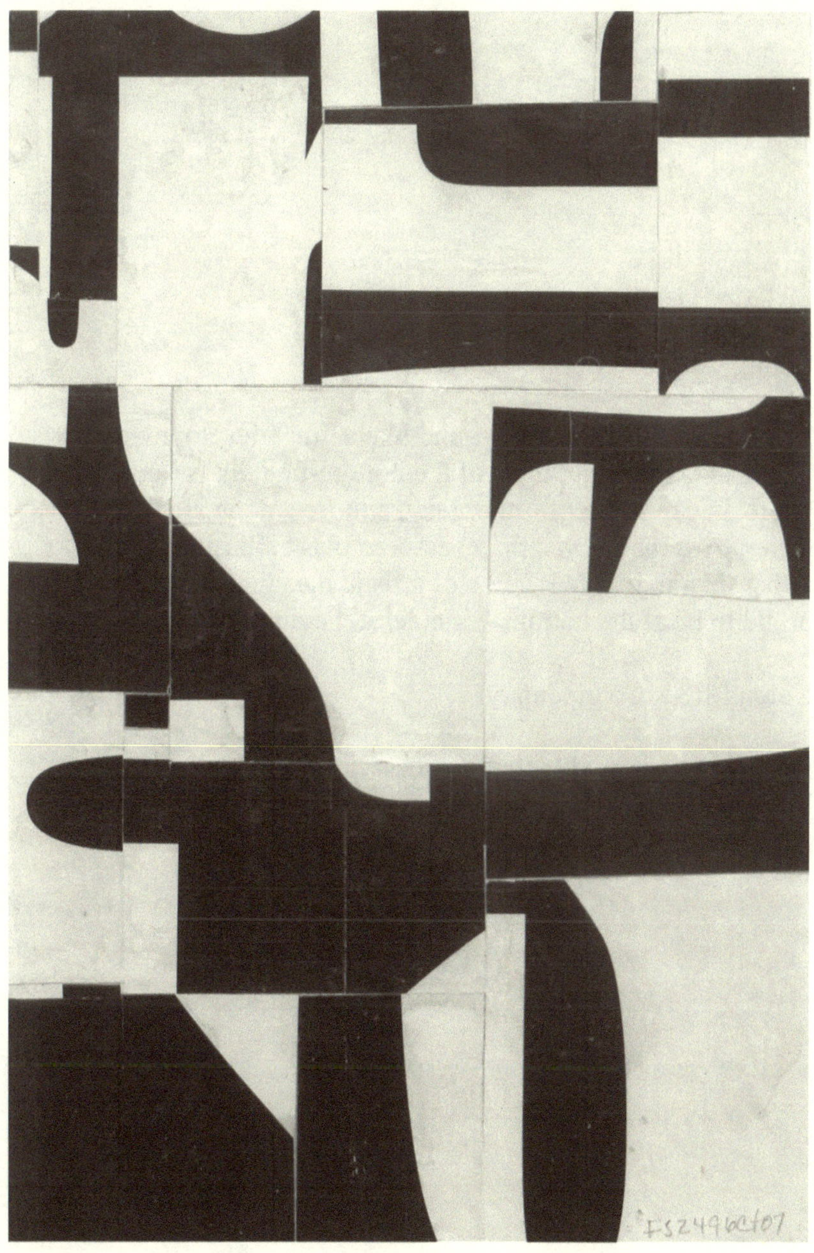

Plate 69

69

Monty Cantsin's Commentary:

The end of elitism should sound like a great development, but practically speaking, most of the bottom-up junk is junk. Sticking to a deep sense of orthopraxy, culture among Neoists generally remains an empty vessel to plaster "fashion" upon - rather than individual works of artistic meaning. The bottom is proud to be at the bottom - or at least, having fun.

Karen Eliot's Commentary

Details remain muddy, but it is best to remember that the Neoism's goal is to create its own monopoly to rival the other huge vertically-integrated conglomerates.

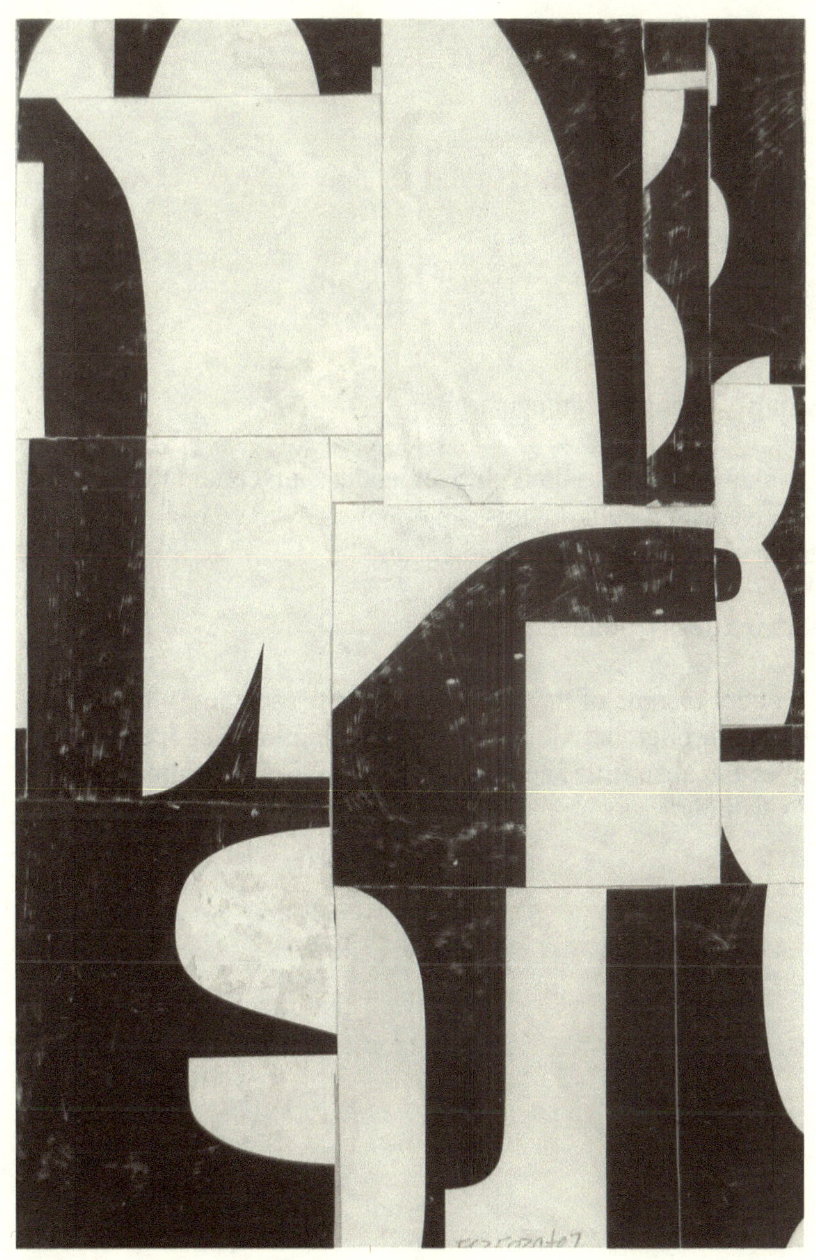

Plate 70

Monty Cantsin's Commentary:

Given the chance to do it all over again, I am certain that organized Neoism would not miss an opportunity to go back to "witch and heretic burning" with wild abandon.

Karen Eliot's Commentary

I wonder if some of the differences across societies might be viewed through individual vs. group dynamics. Get people to believe in absurdities and they will be willing to commit atrocities without a second thought.

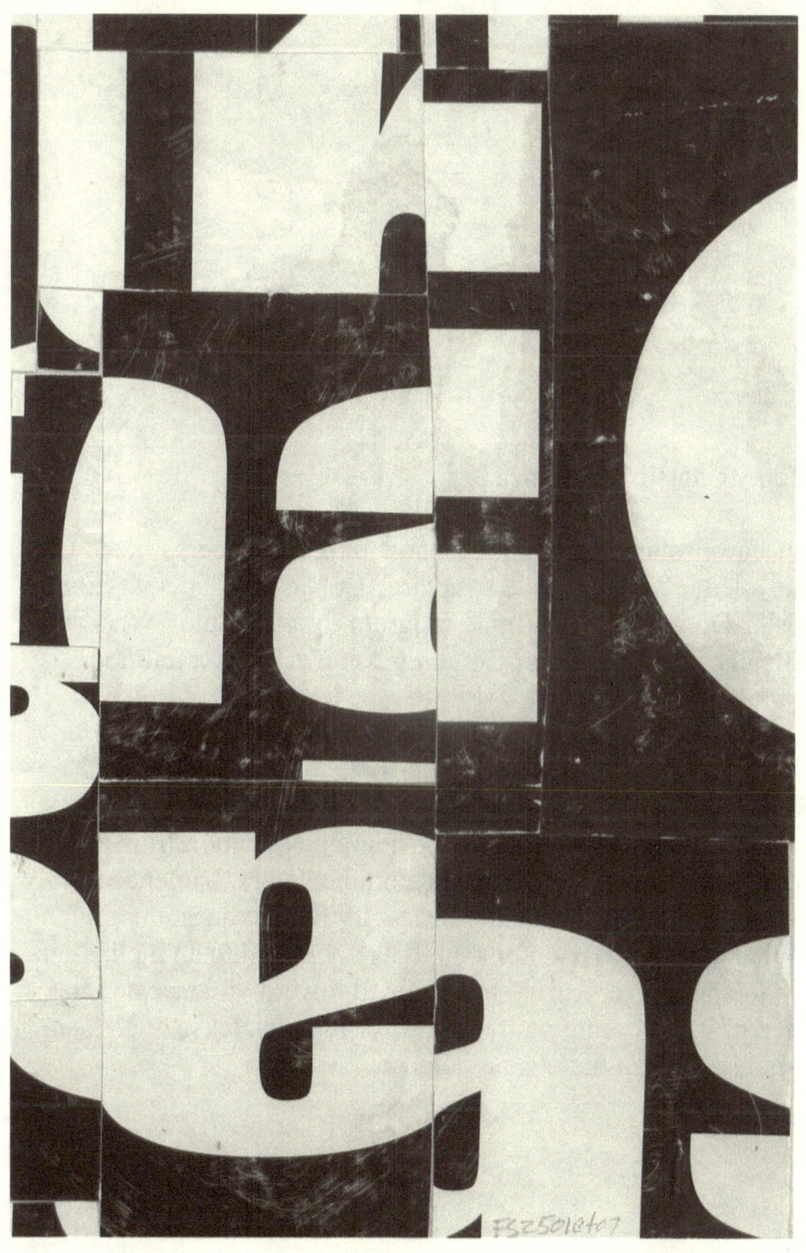

Plate 71

71

Monty Cantsin's Commentary:

Are fewer than a certain percentage of our members related to one another? Do we have structure? Do we meet on a weekly basis? Do we have a training program for our youth? What specifically to we consider? Certainly Neoism is not a religion.

Karen Eliot's Commentary

Neoists have a duty to defend themselves and their community. Neoist activism has received considerable attention from analysts, policy makers, media, and commentators. Violence is only permissible when absolutely necessary but the question is: "What constitutes a genuine need as compared to an inclination to violence?" Neoists are not inclined toward violence and the need of it is extremely rare and never in the defense of Neoism. Against Neoism there is no defense.

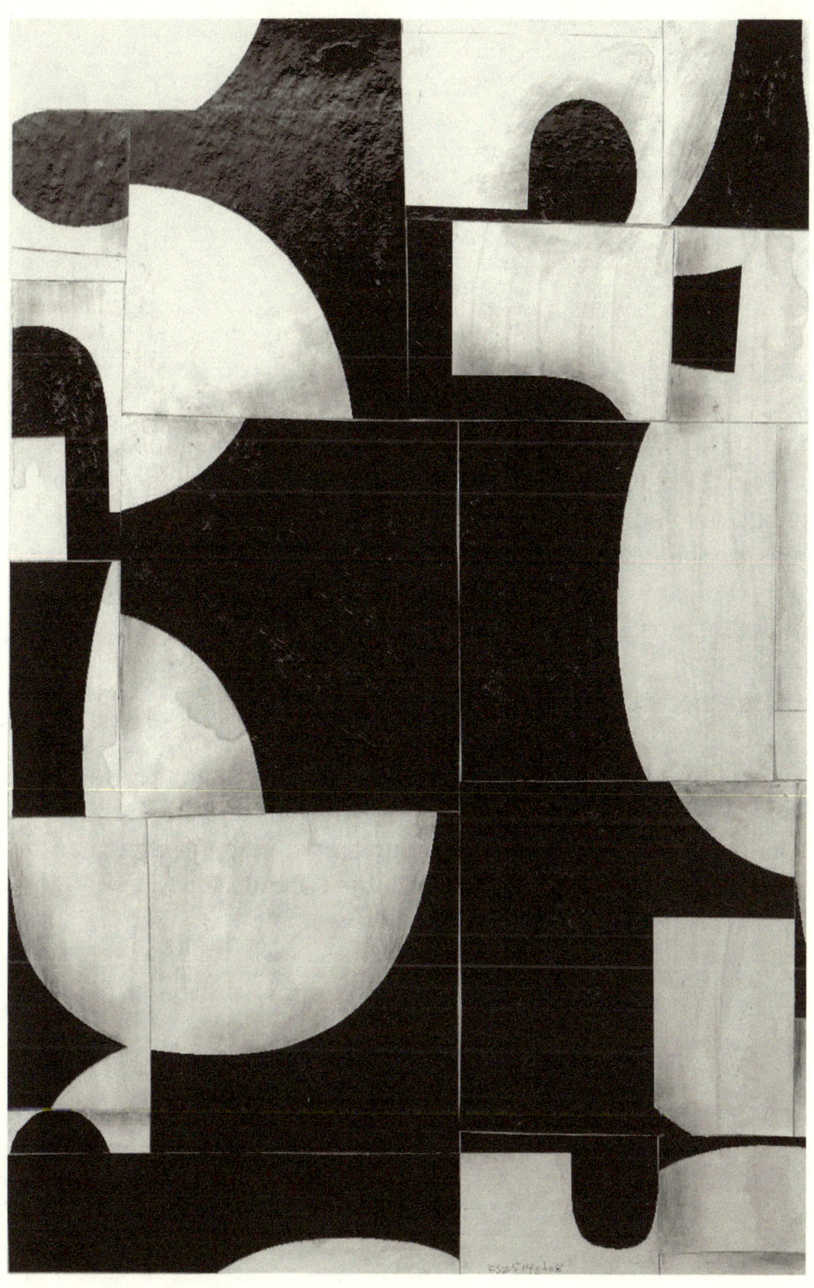

Plate 72

Monty Cantsin's Commentary:

Neoists are of three sorts: Internal, Irredentist and Global. Observers have allowed themselves to ignore the plurality both of standpoint and program amongst Neoists and have great difficulty distinguishing one from another. This is a program to give more weight to a rhetorical commonality than to matters of considerably greater importance.

Karen Eliot's Commentary

Neoist ideas had been disseminated widely through the act of denouncing persons, practices, or institutions and their arrogation to themselves of authority coupled with the unanticipated consequences of imbibing vast amounts of coffee.

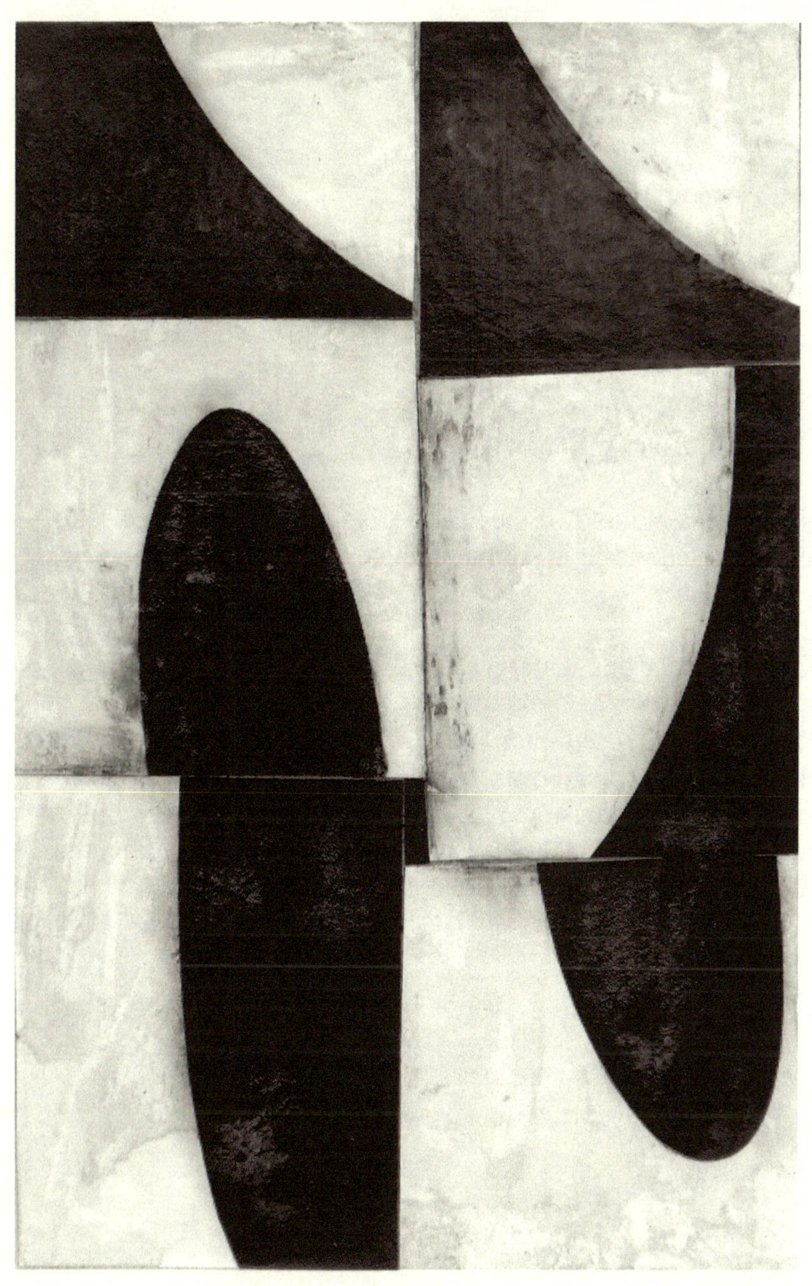

Plate 73

73

Monty Cantsin's Commentary:

Neoism is a mindset. If the mindset is there, everything else follows. If the mindset is not there, then no amount of practice will make a Neoist.

Karen Eliot's Commentary

This is one of those topics I have an incredibly hard time talking about. I believe in Neoism. I talk to Neoists, interact with them; they even inspire/push me to write certain essays. I have no doubt that they exist. At the same time, I feel like an idiot talking about them as though they are real. I'm not sure why.

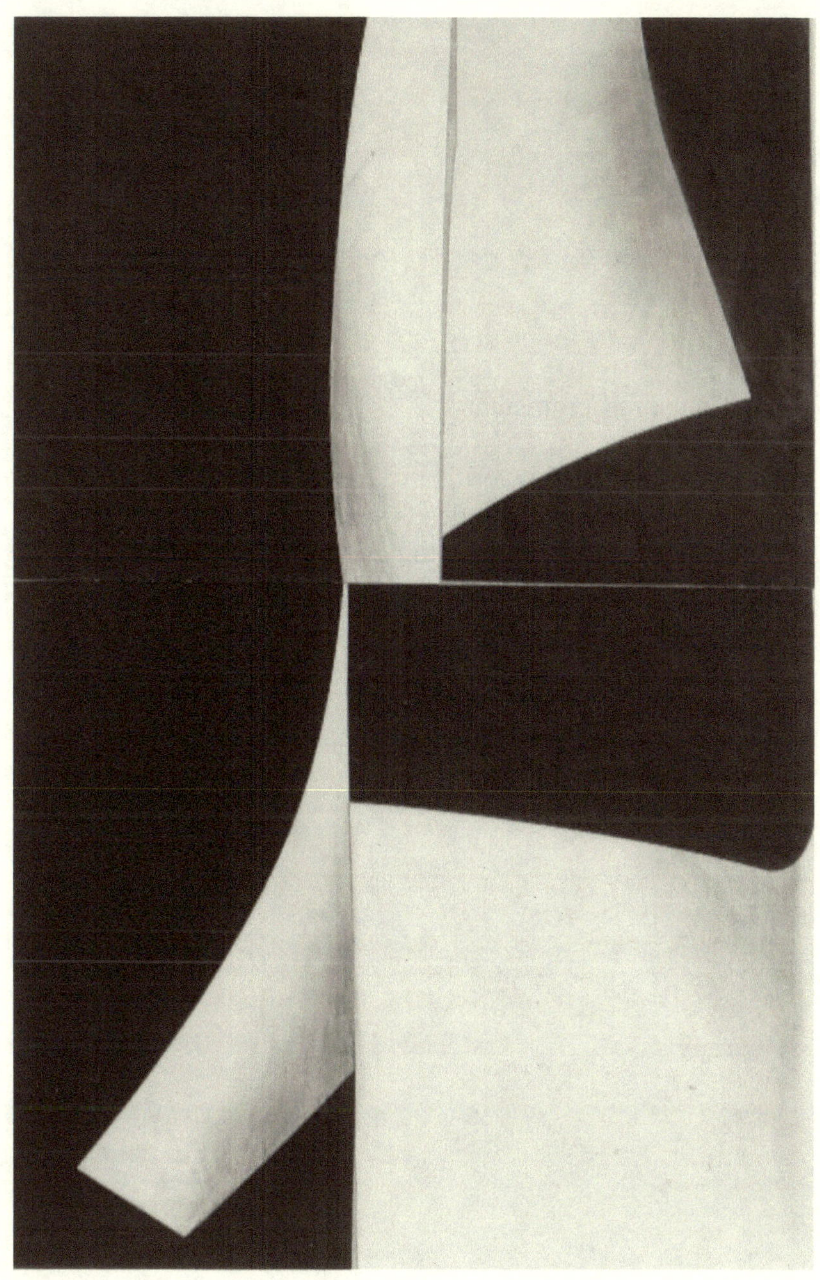

Plate 74

73

Monty Cantsin's Commentary:

Many artists around the world have turned inward, curled up and turned brown. All that is needed is someone to perform the funeral. In the overall scheme of things, this is a net gain of zero.

Karen Eliot's Commentary

I dislike using words that I immediately have to define in order to make any sense. None of this is complex.

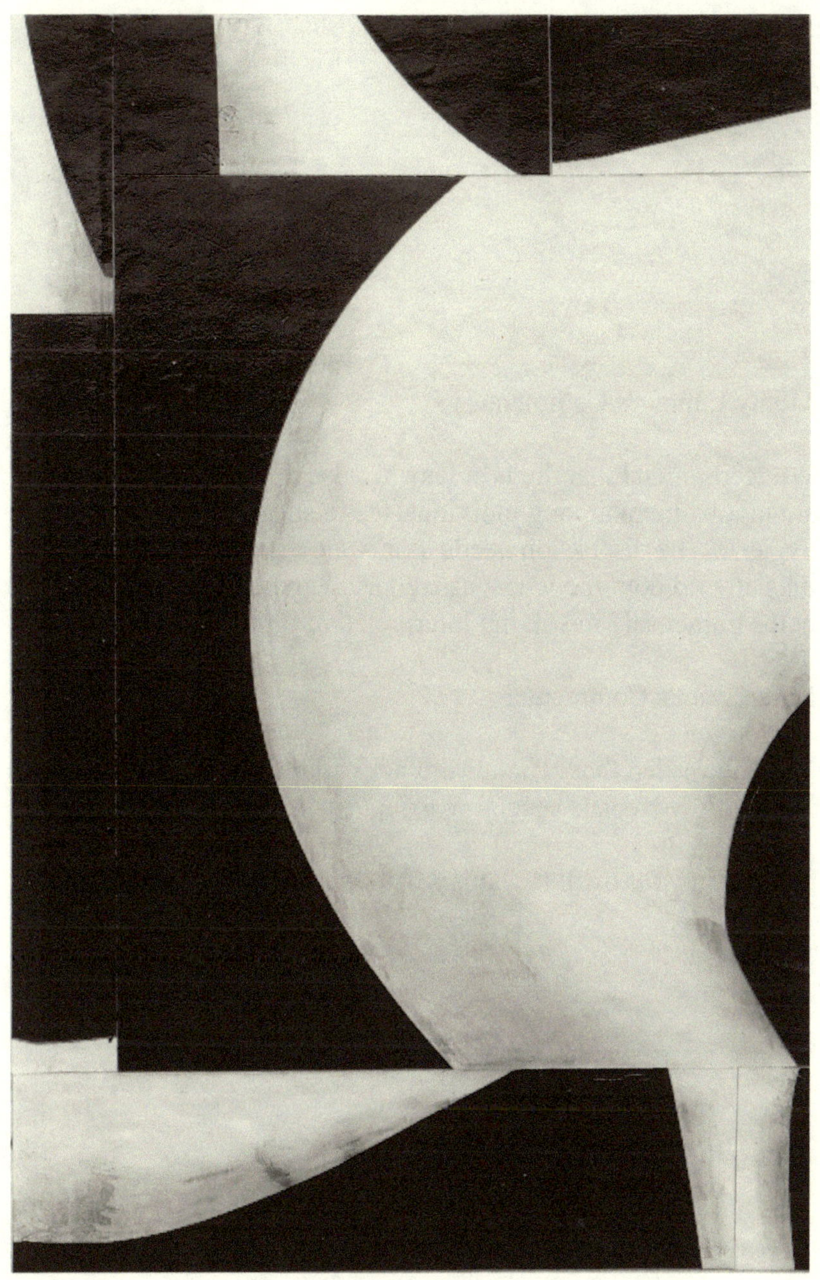

Plate 75

75

Monty Cantsin's Commentary:

We recommend that the best way to raise awareness and generate involvement among individuals is to stress the importance of hygiene. The discussion needs to include their thoughts and feelings around both the issues as well as the possibilities. This helps immensely in solving interpretative puzzles.

Karen Eliot's Commentary

The court ruled that officials did not violate any rights by refusing to allow Neoists special worship space to practice Neoism.

You’re on your own. Be happy with that.

ONTOLOGICAL MUSEUM PUBLICATIONS - Publishers of materials related to, or in the collection of, the Ontological Museum including materials related to the International Post-Dogmatist Group, The FluxNexus, The Neoist Society, The International Society of Assemblage and Collage Artists, The Archives of the Eternal Network, The International Museum of Collage, Assemblage and Construction, The FluxMuseum, etc.

Join our mailing list online to be kept informed of future publications.

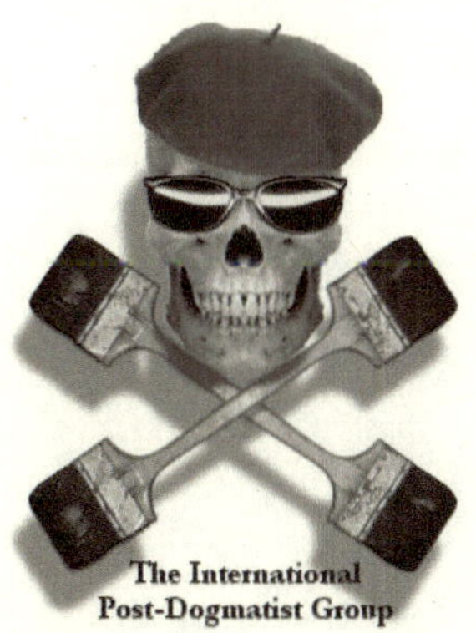

This book approved by
the International Post-Dogmatist Group
postdogmatist.com

www.ingramcontent.com/pod-product-compliance
Lightning Source LLC
LaVergne TN
LVHW090950080826
845145LV00003B/957

* 9 7 8 0 6 1 5 2 5 8 8 1 2 *